THIS

"Did you even give Coralie a chance?"

Charles paused, arrested by Katherine's question, surprised she should have asked it. "More than one," he said.

"And you'll never forgive her." It was a statement more than a question, but he answered.

"No. What she did was unforgivable."

It was the sort of uncompromising reply Katherine had expected him to make, and she knew that he cast her in the same mold as he did Coralie.

"I thought I knew Coralie," she said slowly, "but people change...."

Charles looked unimpressed. "You were willing to help her," he pointed out.

"And I still don't know whether I was right or wrong!" Katherine exclaimed. "You tell me what you want me to know—nothing more."

"That," he said, "is because I don't trust you."

JEAN S. MacLEOD
is also the author of these
Harlequin Romances

966—CRANE CASTLE
990—THE WOLF OF HEIMRA
1016—TWO PATHS
1037—THE TENDER GLORY
1070—THE DRUMMER OF CORRAE
1095—MIST ACROSS THE HILLS
1118—LAMENT FOR LOVE
1150—THE BRIDE OF MINGALAY
1184—THE HOUSE OF OLIVER
1213—THE MOONFLOWER
1254—THE MASTER OF KEILLS
1291—MASTER OF GLENKEITH
1314—SUMMER ISLAND
1339—SLAVE OF THE WIND
1364—ONE LOVE
1414—SOWN IN THE WIND
1440—BLEAK HERITAGE
1466—RETURN TO SPRING
1518—THE LIGHT IN THE TOWER
1552—THE WAY THROUGH THE VALLEY
1613—MOMENT OF DECISION
1693—ADAM'S DAUGHTER
1719—THE RAINBOW DAYS
1845—TIME SUSPENDED
2024—JOURNEY INTO SPRING
2142—ISLAND STRANGER
2191—SEARCH FOR YESTERDAY
2366—BRIEF ENCHANTMENT
2414—BLACK SAND, WHITE SAND
2482—MEETING IN MADRID

Moreton's Kingdom

by

JEAN S. MacLEOD

Harlequin Books

TORONTO • LONDON • LOS ANGELES • AMSTERDAM
SYDNEY • HAMBURG • PARIS • STOCKHOLM • ATHENS • TOKYO

Original hardcover edition published in 1981
by Mills & Boon Limited

ISBN 0-373-02499-1

Harlequin Romance first edition September 1982

Printed in U.S.A.

CHAPTER ONE

The flat was grossly overcrowded, and Katherine wished she hadn't come. Most of the people there were strangers to her, although she had lived and worked in London for the past two years, but she had accepted the invitation on impulse on the eve of going on holiday because she had suddenly become aware of a loneliness she could not explain away merely by telling herself that she had given everything to her career during these past two years, only to find herself out of a job because her elderly boss had died and his younger successor had brought his own private secretary into the office with him.

Henry Bellinger had been more like a father to her than an indulgent employer and his breezy American charm had won her over at their very first meeting, claiming her allegiance thereafter as a matter of course, so that his death had been a great blow to her. In the two crowded years in which they had worked together neither of them had taken a holiday, and Katherine had been deeply touched when she had been left sufficient money to go away for a while and enjoy herself, as Henry had put it in his will.

Looking around her, she wondered idly how so many people had been able to crowd into an average-sized room. It seemed that they were all talking at cross purposes and the resultant noise was deafening.

'Hullo!' someone observed at her elbow. 'I think we ought to know each other.'

She turned to find a girl about her own age squeezing between two of their fellow guests to confront her with an engaging smile which was vaguely familiar.

'You'll have to prompt me,' she said.

'St Monica's, Hayley Hill.' The smile was wide and

friendly. 'You're Katherine Rivers, aren't you? We went to school together.'

'Coralie Edgar!' Katherine remembered. 'Of course!'

The years slid away—seven years, to be exact—and she was back at St Monica's, a lanky schoolgirl who had looked up to Coralie Edgar from afar, Coralie who had been the captain of hockey and head girl, to boot, someone so far removed from the introspective fourth former of those bygone days that she might have existed in another world.

'You *do* remember!' Coralie smiled. 'And I felt sure I couldn't be mistaken.'

'Are you living in London?' Katherine asked the obvious question because she couldn't think of anything more original to say. She was hopeless at the sort of light conversation which accompanied such encounters and usually ended in a broken sentence with people drifting off to speak with someone else. 'I suppose you are or you wouldn't be here. I was told it was a local get-together.'

Coralie nodded.

'You could call it that,' she agreed. 'I don't know very many people here, either.' Her blue eyes scanned the other occupants of the room with a suggestion of apprehension in their depths. 'It's frightening, isn't it?' she ran on. 'All these people gabbling away about nothing in particular to other people they hardly know.'

Katherine laughed.

'I was thinking that,' she admitted. 'Eventually, I find myself without a voice, but that might just be because I'm out of practice.'

Coralie nodded, sipping some of the wine from an overfull glass.

'I generally spill it all over myself,' she admitted ruefully, 'or over someone else!' Once again the anxious blue eyes scanned the room. 'I came here looking for someone,' she confessed, 'but he hasn't put in an appearance. He's the unpredictable sort, and it was more or less a business meeting, anyway.'

'I'm sorry,' said Katherine.

'Don't be!' The blue eyes were studying her closely. 'Tell me what you've been doing since you left St Monica's.'

Katherine smiled.

'That isn't a very tall order,' she said. 'I was a secretary for three years, and then I went to work with an American firm as private secretary to the boss.'

Coralie's eyebrows lifted in evident surprise.

'Well, well!' she said almost patronisingly. 'Do you travel a lot?'

'I used to when Mr Bellinger was alive.'

'Your boss?'

Katherine nodded.

'I'm taking a holiday now because he left me enough money to buy a car and go off for a while,' she explained.

'Where will you go?' Coralie asked the question with a suggestion of indifference in her pleasant voice.

'I've made up my mind to go to Scotland,' Katherine told her. 'It's years since I've been there and I've always wanted to go back.'

'I can't think why,' said Coralie. 'I used to live there.' Her mouth hardened into a thin line, stealing away some of her beauty. 'I married a Scot, but that's past tense now.'

Katherine glanced at the bare third finger of her left hand.

'We're divorced,' Coralie said without bitterness. 'It didn't work out.'

'I'm sorry.' Katherine wasn't quite sure what to say next or if anything was really expected of her. 'It must have left—a tremendous gap in your life,' she added sympathetically.

'Not really.' The blue eyes were still searching the room. 'You see, I had my career. I never realised how much it meant to me till I was on my own again. In some ways it was sheer bliss to be free. In others——' Coralie hesitated, seeming to look at Katherine fully for the first time, her blue eyes faintly calculating. 'In others,' she repeated deliberately, 'it was not so easy. I had a child, you see—a small boy who meant a great deal to us both.'

Katherine waited, but that seemed as far as Coralie's explanations were prepared to go.

'Don't say you're sorry,' she added with a hard little movement of her mouth which was scarcely a smile. 'It was just one of these things, and I made my own decision.'

'Tell me about your career,' Katherine prompted. 'You were always clever at school.'

It was still as Coralie Edgar that she remembered this lovely, talented girl, and now it seemed that Coralie was in need of sympathy, at least.

Coralie's eyes lit up.

'It was always an obsession with me,' she confessed. 'You know—something I had to do. Even before art school, designing came easy to me, and afterwards I was on my way. I'd got at least a foot in the door before I married, and now I know I shouldn't have given it up. Not entirely,' she added firmly. 'It was such a waste of training, a sort of betrayal of my given talents, if you like, and yet I suppose I was in love and marriage was the ultimate goal. Are you married, Katie?' she asked inquisitively.

She had used the old name as if they had been the closest of friends all these years ago, and Katherine smiled a little as she shook her head.

'I've never been asked,' she said.

'That's hard to believe,' returned Coralie, studying her more closely. 'You were never a beauty at school—always too thin, if I remember—but you had a quality about you, a remoteness, perhaps, which was interesting. Without that titian hair of yours and your serious look you would be ordinary, but as it is——' She surveyed Katherine critically. 'Have you ever thought of modelling?'

Katherine shook her head.

'I'm happy enough as I am,' she said. 'I'll have to look

for another job when my holiday is over, of course, but I think I ought to stick to the work I know.'

Surprisingly Coralie drew her aside, finding a vacant space beside the wall.

'I'm in a spot, Katie,' she confided. 'The most awful predicament, in fact.' Tears filled her eyes, threatening to spill over as she rushed on: 'I'm not an emotional sort of person as a rule, but my ex-husband is making things difficult for me at present. I love my child, and he's trying to kidnap him.'

'Surely not!' Katherine exclaimed. 'If he loved you——'

Coralie shrugged.

'That's all in the past,' she declared. 'He's completely embittered now and I can't pretend that I'm still in love with him, but I won't let him have my child. Sandy is shy and terribly sensitive. I need him near me, but the fact is that if I have to further my career by going abroad I could easily lose him. I would have to be away from London from time to time and I couldn't take him with me.' She paused, drawing in a deep breath. 'If only someone—some stranger—could get him to the Lake District for me, my sister would look after him till all this blows over.'

'Hide him, do you mean?' Katherine felt aghast.

'In a way, Katie, I really do care about him,' Coralie protested as her carefully-manicured fingers tightened on Katherine's arm. 'You must have been *sent* to help me,' she added. 'Will you do it?'

Torn between surprise and an odd sort of pity for her former schoolfellow, Katherine hesitated. She was the person on the spot as far as Coralie was concerned, but what did she really know about this girl who had made such an outrageous suggestion? They had never been friends. Coralie had lived in a world apart, the brilliant senior pupil who had taken everything in her stride—head girl, captain of this and that, there had been no question about her superiority, yet here she was confessing with tears in her eyes that her marriage had been unsuccessful and she could not cope with the aftermath of parting, that she was virtually afraid. It was evident that her child meant a great deal to her, but not quite so much as a brilliant career.

Wondering why she should have any doubts about Coralie's priorities, she could only think of the 'intensely shy' little boy and feel a tremendous pity both for Coralie and the man she had married.

'What about Sandy?' she asked apprehensively.

'He's only three and a bit and a perfect darling,' Sandy's mother said. 'He'd go with you like a shot.'

It seemed strange to Katherine that a child of that age should transfer his affections so easily to a stranger, but possibly Coralie knew her own son best.

'Will you do it?' she begged. 'I have to know right away. There's really no time to lose.'

Almost forced into acceptance, Katherine said reluctantly:

'I'm leaving in the morning. Surely that's very little time for you to prepare?'

'It's perfect!' Coralie declared. 'Katie, you've no idea how much this means to me. I have to go to New York in a day or two and he'll be safe with my sister. She's an artist of sorts, with a cottage near Bassenthwaite. I don't know why she lives there, because it must be about the loneliest place on earth, but it seems to suit her. Every now and then she comes to London for a showing of her paintings at one or other of the galleries and makes a lot of money. We meet then, but she hasn't been here for some time. We're close, of course, and she'll take Sandy for as long as I need to leave him.'

'I really ought to meet Sandy,' said Katherine. 'It's such short notice. After all, he'd be going away with a complete stranger.'

'I told you not to worry about that,' Coralie persisted with a slight edge to her voice. 'He's completely amenable and he adores his aunt. It will only be for a day and you're travelling north, anyway. The Lake District is not so very far out of your way.'

'No,' Katherine agreed readily enough. 'I had some idea of making Windermere my first stop, as a matter of fact.'

'Then it wouldn't be too far for you to go on to Bassenthwaite,' Coralie reflected with relief. 'Do this for me, Katie, and I'll be eternally grateful,' she added, drawing in a deep breath.

'I meant to leave early tomorrow morning,' said Katherine, still not fully convinced that she should do this thing. 'The traffic out of London is lighter then and I'm not the world's best driver.'

'That's ideal,' Coralie declared. 'I can be at your place as early as you like. It will be better that way,' she concluded. 'I feel I'm being watched.'

'Are you sure?' Katherine asked, finding an old envelope with her address on it.

'Absolutely.' Coralie took the envelope and placed it in her own handbag. 'I trust you. I need your help. Afterwards I'll make it up to you, somehow. Just get Sandy safely to Bassenthwaite and I'll be eternally grateful. There's no more I can say.'

Looking swiftly about her, she made for the door as if she were actually being followed.

Katherine stood where she was, feeling that she had bitten off more than she could chew, even if the undertaking was only for a day. Kidnapping was an ugly word which she had never really thought about before, and surely the child's father must be some kind of monster to inflict such a situation on someone he had once loved. Yet these things did happen, she supposed, when emotions got out of hand and people inflicted heartache on one another out of another kind of love. Affection for his child was as much a man's prerogative as a woman's, but this time it seemed that Coralie's ex-husband was stepping outside the law.

When she looked across the crowded room she was immediately aware of a tall man making his way towards her. Standing head and shoulders above the other guests, he looked almost out of place in the crowded flat with its brilliant lighting and effusive, chattering groups talking far too loudly and laughing a great deal. He was a man accustomed to being out of doors, she thought fleetingly, although he was dressed conventionally enough in a city suit. The fact that he was appraising her with a steady stare made her turn her head away. He would be a man who would go for what he wanted without hesitation, and she was hardly surprised to find him at her elbow when she turned towards the door.

Suddenly her heart seemed to miss a beat as a pair of enigmatic grey eyes fastened on her own.

'This is Charles,' their hostess introduced them in the modern idiom of no surnames. 'Charles—Katherine. You ought to have all sorts of things in common,' she added vaguely. 'You're both Scots and terribly attached to your native land.'

'Does that mean you live in Scotland?' the tall man asked, his scrutiny demanding now.

'No, but I go there as often as I can,' Katherine admitted, liking him although the grey eyes had hardened as he assessed her. 'Millie said you were a Scot and I think I'd almost guessed that. You look—intolerant of the London scene.'

'Not entirely.' The searching grey eyes were still intently on hers. 'I have to come here occasionally on business, but I prefer the freedom of what Millie calls "our native land". Which part of Scotland do you claim?'

'Nowhere specific at the moment. My parents are dead and I've been working in London for the past two years with frequent visits abroad, but I was born in Perthshire and I thought I'd go back there, if only for a visit.'

'Which means you'll be leaving London in the near future,' he suggested. 'It doesn't give us much time to become acquainted.'

A faint colour dyed her cheeks and she was suddenly conscious of her quickened heartbeats, aware that she had never been so immediately attracted to anyone before.

'I wonder if I'll regret the fact,' she said.

Smiling up at him, she was aware of a sudden cold reserve in him, a calculated questioning of the account she had given of herself.

'Can I get you another drink?' he asked, relieving her of her empty glass.

'I really must go.' There was an element of self-protection in her refusal. 'I have an early start in the morning.'

'Going where?' He was standing between her and the door almost as if he would bar her only means of escape.

'Nowhere in particular,' she lied warily for no very clear reason. 'If I'm driving any distance I like to get away before the business traffic thickens, and the only way to do that is to get up at dawn!'

'Do you mean to drive far?' he asked idly, setting down his own empty glass. 'I presume you have your own car?'

'Not here.' She had evaded the primary question. 'I live near enough to walk back to my own flat.'

'It's raining,' he said. 'Let me drive you home.'

There seemed to be no point in refusing his offer since she was ill equipped for walking in the rain.

'I didn't bring a coat,' she confessed. 'It was fine enough when I set out.'

He guided her towards the door, where they shook hands with Millie Downhill, who had miraculously remembered their Christian names if not their surnames.

'Come again!' Millie said breezily. 'I'm always giving parties.'

On their way down in the lift Katherine wondered what relationship there could possibly be between the silent man at her side and the ebullient Millie who was 'always giving parties'. Her own acquaintance was a second-hand affair, and she had been talked into going to Millie's flat by a former colleague who had promptly left her to her own devices as soon as they had arrived, but possibly Charles's friendship with their hostess was of longer duration.

'Is Millie an old friend?' she asked curiously. 'I thought we both looked a bit like fishes out of water up there!'

'Millie used to work for me in Edinburgh,' he said, 'but she drifted to London in search of a higher salary. I came along tonight to please her—and to look for somebody,' he added.

'Whom you didn't find.' She turned towards him as the lift reached the ground floor. 'Perhaps you should go back,' she suggested, fully convinced that he had been searching for a woman. 'I'm sure the party's only just starting.'

He opened the gate.

'I've had all the noisy chatter I need for one evening,' he said.

'But the friend you hoped to meet?' Katherine persisted. 'She might expect you to be there.'

'I know where she lives,' he said.

So it had been a woman he had been waiting for! She walked ahead of him across the carpeted entrance hall.

'I really can make my own way home,' she said.

He opened the stout main door without answering her.

'It's still raining,' he pointed out.

His car was parked farther down the block, a grey Rover splendidly British in its solidarity, like its enigmatic owner.

'How far?' he asked.

'Only a little way on the far side of the Park.'

It was no great distance, as she had promised, and they reached her destination within a quarter of an hour despite the thickening flow of traffice. It was still raining as Charles drew up at the kerb.

'Thank you,' she said. 'I'm very grateful—Charles.'

He smiled at her tentative use of his Christian name.

'Charles Moreton,' he replied as she had expected him to do.

'I'm Katherine Rivers,' she said. 'Generally known as Kate!'

'Are you an obliging friend, Kate?' he asked unexpectedly. 'Someone who would do a good turn without thinking twice about it?'

'I don't know.' Her reply to the challenging question was slightly doubtful. 'I suppose I would consider it unless it was really urgent.'

'Ah,' he said, but that was all.

He helped her out of the car, climbed the three stone steps to her front door and held out his hand for her key.

'I'd ask you in,' Katherine said hastily, 'but I'm rather tired.'

'And you're off early in the morning,' he supplied for her. 'All right, Kate, I can take a hint when it's so obvious. We'll meet again, would you say?'

'I—yes, that would be nice.' She had given way to impulse because she did not want to let him go for some perverse reason which she would not admit even to herself. 'Unless you forget,' she added, throwing down her own challenge.

He took her by the shoulders, the grey eyes searching hers.

'I won't forget,' he said grimly. 'Goodnight, Kate!' He pressed his lips firmly on hers.

The kiss was short and almost defiant, and it seared through her like a flame. She had been kissed before, but never quite like this, for the hard pressure of his lips seemed to have drained away all her vitality, leaving her limply at this man's mercy. Why had he done it? What reason had he to make her feel at a loss?

When she reached her own flat she went straight to the window which overlooked the tree-lined avenue without switching on the lights. The grey car was still parked at the kerb, its owner standing beside it surveying his surroundings with a contemplative air. He turned away almost immediately, however, so there was really no reason why her heart should suddenly be thumping in her breast at the memory of a careless goodnight kiss.

Best to forget about Charles Moreton, she decided, since she was never likely to meet him again.

In the morning she was awakened by the sun filtering through the unlined curtains of her room to fill it with a mellow, diffused light as she swung her feet to the floor. The panic thought that she had overslept took her swiftly to her dressing-table, but it was only five o'clock when she consulted her watch. Quickly she drew back the curtains, looking over the tree tops of the tiny square to a sky washed blue and shining by the rain of the night before. The plane trees in brave new bud stood out against it, palely green in the early light, and her heart rose in anticipation of a perfect day. Always, as she prepared for a journey, she had experienced a quick surge of excitement, and this day was no different except for the fact that she had undertaken a strange assignment on the spur of the moment the night before.

In the penetrating light of a new day it seemed absurd that she had accepted full responsibility for a small boy whom she had never met because his mother believed that he was about to be kidnapped by the man she had recently divorced.

As she cooked a hasty breakfast and packed the few remaining articles of clothing she would need for her holiday she wondered about Coralie Edgar and her child, anticipating a tearful scene when they came to part, but perhaps they wouldn't come at all. Coralie might change her mind when she thought carefully about all that parting could entail. She had expressed her love for Sandy in no uncertain terms, but perhaps anxiety for his safety would bring her eventually to the flat.

The door bell rang at six o'clock. Katherine was tidying up in the kitchen, making sure that she had emptied the refrigerator and leaving nothing to go stale during the three weeks or so that she intended to be away, and she opened the door with a milk bottle in her hand.

Coralie was standing outside with a small boy by the hand and she found herself looking at Sandy with swift compassion because he appeared to be completely bewildered. His mother had called him docile, presenting a picture of a child who would do exactly as he was told, causing her no trouble at all, but she had not been prepared for the lost look in Sandy's wide blue eyes. He seemed completely at a loss as he clung to Coralie's hand, gloved fingers tightening compulsively about it as he contemplated Katherine for the first time.

In a tone that Katherine disliked immediately, Coralie said:

'Here we are, darling! This is the kind lady who's going to take you in her car to stay with Aunt Hattie for a while. You know how much you love Aunt Hattie,' she prompted when Sandy made no immediate reply, 'and you'll see the dogs again and the chickens. That'll be nice, won't it?'

Eyes clearer and even more blue than her own were lifted to her face, searching eyes full of a deep wistfulness which immediately touched Katherine's heart.

'Are you sure about this?' she asked her early-morning visitor beneath her breath as Coralie ushed her son across the threshold.

'Quite sure.' There was complete determination and a noticeable harshness in Coralie's tone. 'You're not thinking of backing out, are you, after promising?'

'I wouldn't do that.' Katherine was still looking at the child. 'It was just that I wondered how he would feel being handed over to a complete stranger.'

'He's not old enough to "feel" anything in the way you mean,' Coralie declared, 'and he's used to being in different places most of the time. He's been divided neatly down the centre between my husband and me. It's the sort of situation that makes for docility, don't you think?'

Katherine took Sandy by the hand, leading him to the window to look down at the trees where a light wind was stirring their branches.

'When you see the milk-float coming we'll put all the bottles out for the milkman,' she suggested. 'I have to tell him I won't need any more milk.'

Sandy stood dutifully by the window while his mother followed Katherine into the kitchen.

'He knows you're going to take him,' she said briskly, 'so you needn't pamper him. Believe me, it's safer this way because his father is determined to have him all the time. Our marriage couldn't have lasted. I should have expected it to founder, sooner or later, but Sandy has complicated matters. My ex-husband wants him because he's the heir to a great deal of money. His uncle settled a considerable sum on him when he was one year old and my ex is determined to have full control of it.'

'But surely you were given custody,' Katherine protested.

The blue eyes widened.

'Of course,' said Coralie. 'What else?'

'Then you're safe enough under the law.'

'You don't know my ex-husband.' Coralie turned away. 'He's a law unto himself, and once Sandy is in Scotland he could make it difficult for me. Scots law is different in some respects.'

She was almost in tears, and Katherine felt immediately sorry for her.

'This is really serious,' she said. 'Why don't you go to the police?'

Coralie hesitated, but only for a second.

'I couldn't face another court case,' she said. 'You've no idea how soul-destroying it can be to have your private life dragged in front of a judge who takes everything you say with a pinch of salt.' She glanced at the clock. 'I have to go,' she decided. 'I have a business appointment at nine o'clock. I'm a working girl again. You've no idea how good that feels after all I've been through.'

'I'll have to have your sister's address,' Katherine reminded her. 'I dare say you've spoken to her.'

'She isn't on the phone, but I've scribbled her address down somewhere.' Coralie searched in her handbag. 'You won't have any difficulty finding the cottage. You turn off the M6 and go by Ambleside and Keswick. That way you can avoid Penrith when you go north again. It's lovely countryside if you haven't been there before.'

She produced a slip of paper with an address written on it and a sketchy diagram of the locality. Skiddaw she had marked with a little pyramid and there was another for the Saddleback, but apart from that the road seemed to wind vaguely northwards and eastwards in the general direction of Carlisle.

'I'll find it.' Katherine felt that she would be safer with her ordinary road-map. 'Are you quite sure you want me to do this, Coralie?' she asked on a final impulse. 'We don't really know each other very well.'

'That's beside the point. We were at school together and that's assurance enough as far as I'm concerned.' The older girl's expression sharpened a little. 'You couldn't possibly back out on me now,' she pleaded. 'Not after promising.'

It would only be one day, Katherine thought again, and a delightful small boy would be a good companion on the road.

Coralie parted with her son with surprisingly little sentiment.

'You'll do everything Katie tells you, won't you, darling?' She squeezed his hand. 'Then you'll be with Aunt Hattie for a while. You'll like that, won't you?' She pressed a swift kiss against his cold little cheek. 'Be a good boy!'

There had been no promise that she would collect him in the very near future, nothing for a bewildered child to hang on to when she had gone. I wish I hadn't promised to help, Katherine thought. It's all so cold and terribly unfeeling.

After Coralie had gone she finished her packing while Sandy stood by the window in silence, watching for the milk-float, and when it finally came round the corner he helped her to carry the empty milk bottles to the foot of the stairs, standing in the doorway while she paid the man. Already the morning traffic had become a thin trickle and it was time they had made a start if they were to be through London before the incoming tide of vehicles swamped them altogether.

Coralie had deposited a tartan holdall just inside the flat door, and Sandy looked somehow pathetic as he lugged it on to the landing.

'Don't forget your anorak,' Katherine reminded him briskly to hide her concern.

She had parked her car on the far side of the road and she bundled her small companion in after she had checked that there was a rug if he wanted to sleep. Did little boys of three and a bit need an afternoon rest? She looked at the silent child by her side as she drove off, supposing that nature would supply an adequate answer to her ignorance.

Sandy had fallen asleep before they had reached Birmingham, propped up comfortably with his seat belt and the travelling-rug. Their conversation had consisted chiefly of quick observations about passing vehicles and the colour of cars, which he seemed to recognise, the fact that he was able to count up to twenty surprising her a little.

While he slept, Katherine had more time to think of the remainder of their journey, realising with a vague feeling of regret that it was already half over. She would miss Sandy when she finally deposited him at Beck Cottage where his aunt would be waiting for him. Evidently he knew Hattie Edgar very well because he had smiled each time her name was mentioned, a fact which Katherine accepted as a form of reassurance, although why she should need convincing that everything would turn out right for Sandy she didn't know.

Uneasily she looked down at the fair head cradled in her ancient travelling-rug. He seemed so young and vulnerable lying there with a half-smile curving his lips as if his unconscious thoughts were completely happy ones, but it seemed useless to tear her own heart apart with needless pitying. When they reached Beck Cottage her responsibility for this enchanting scrap of humanity would be over. An odd regret continued to tug at her heart, but she shrugged it aside deliberately in order to concentrate on her driving.

When Sandy opened his eyes again she was ready to smile at him.

'Are you very hungry?' she asked. 'I am, so we'll stop at the very next café for something to eat.'

'Chips?' he asked expectantly.

'If you like them we'll have chips.'

'An' lemonade?'

'Milk would be nicer. You could have lemonade later on.'

He nodded, not showing any disappointment at her verdict.

'Or we might even be able to get some orange juice,' she suggested.

'Yes.'

He was too docile, Katherine thought with sudden irritation, too ready to agree to any suggestion made to him by an adult world which had little room for a small boy.

I shouldn't think these things, she told herself immediately. After all, Sandy is well provided for, with an uncle who's cared enough about him to leave him a small fortune, protecting his future in a material sense, at least.

'Can you watch out for a notice that has spoons and knives and forks on it?' she asked to amuse him. 'There should be one quite soon and that's where we'll stop.'

Refreshed by his sleep, Sandy entered into the spirit of the game she had suggested, eyes brightly excited as he pointed to the sign.

'There!' he said. 'I'm hungry for chips.'

He ate heartily, consuming his helping of fish and chips in record time while a smiling waitress stood by to take his further order.

'Do they all eat like this?' Katherine laughed. 'Surely that wasn't just a child's portion?'

'What we lose on the swings we gain on the roundabouts!' the girl laughed. 'Some kids just peck at their food, but I like to see them with a healthy appetite. There's apple pie and cream to follow, or strawberry ice,' she added expectantly.

Katherine chose the apple pie, but Sandy had seen a child at an adjacent table with a large helping of strawberry ice-cream in a glass, so there was no question about his choice. He ate it in silence, licking the spoon reflectively while Katherine drank her coffee. Sandy was opening out.

When they rejoined the trunk road Katherine suggested another game.

'We'll watch all the cars coming towards us and count the blue ones,' she said. 'Only blue ones, starting from now!'

Once the decision had been made it was surprising how many blue cars there were on the road going the opposite way. Sandy reached his counting limit of twenty in under an hour and they had to start all over again, but the game had proved successful and Katherine kept it up with a show of enthusiasm which matched the sparkle in Sandy's eyes.

Once or twice, as she glanced through her driving mirror, she saw a blue car catching up with them, but that wasn't part of the game. All the cars had to be going the other way.

Perhaps it was then that she became aware of a second car keeping pace with them, a grey car which could have passed her easily enough, she thought absently.

Before they reached Kendal they stopped for tea. Sandy had slept on the seat beside her for the second time when the car-spotting game had become too repetitive and she felt that he must be ready for something more to eat. The grey car followed them off the highway, although she did not see its occupants get out because it parked some way ahead of her as she hurried Sandy into the Ladies' Room before ordering their second meal of the day.

'I don't think we should have more chips,' she said. 'How about an egg?'

'I like eggs,' Sandy nodded, 'but I like chips better.'

'H'mm! Well, eggs it is,' Katherine decided. 'I dare say you can have chips tomorrow when you're at the cottage.'

It was amazing how heartily he ate, she thought, realising that he had no fads about his food, and when they were on the road again she suggested another game.

'Cows in a field,' she said. 'How many you can count as we pass!'

'Brown ones?' he asked.

'Any colour. Most of them will be brown with white patches on their sides.'

At the next junction she left the trunk road and a grey car turned with her. The same grey car which had followed her into the motorway café to park ahead of her.

Her heart began to thump at the thought of being followed, but she managed to assure herself that it was no more than a coincidence.

The Lake District was at its enchanting best as she drove slowly along the narrower, winding roads which skirted the mountains to reveal vast stretches of silver water cradled in deep dales where the sunlight slanted between ancient trees and the clouds sailed high in the clear blue sky. She was travelling west now, several miles out of her way, but what did it really matter? She had no fixed schedule, planning to enjoy herself by moving from place to place at will, with no ultimate destination in mind, which was the best way to see and appreciate her native land. If she reached the Trossachs and returned by the east coast in the three weeks she had allowed herself she would be well satisfied, and the detour into the Lake District which she was making now was one which she might have taken anyway.

Glancing down at her small charge, she thought how easily Sandy had fitted into her scheme of things and how much she would miss him after tomorrow.

At Keswick they stopped for a while to watch the sailing boats skimming across the smooth surface of Derwentwater and Sandy skipped along the shore road, glad to be free, but as soon as it was time to go on, to renew their journey, he climbed back into the car and sat solemnly upright beside her with his eyes on the road. Their journey was almost over.

'I wish you were coming all the way with me,' Katherine said impulsively, 'but soon you'll be with your Aunt Hattie and you can tell her all about the games we played.'

Sandy nodded.

'Could you stay?' he asked, the blue eyes raised enquiringly to hers. 'Could you maybe stay a week an' I could show you the dogs an' the hens.'

Katherine bit her lip.

'I wish I could,' she said, 'but perhaps Aunt Hattie will have other plans.'

Involuntarily she thought of a pursuing car, although there was no sign of one as they drove off on the Bassenthwaite road. On the horizon Skiddaw dominated the view and soon the lake appeared, shining darkly in the last of the sunlight.

At the next village she stopped to ask directions, knowing that they must be near their destination, but as she slowed down a grey car appeared in her driving mirror, pulling out to overtake her, and suddenly her heartbeats quickened, although she had had no more than a passing glimpse of a dark head turned in profile as the car pulled ahead of her to disappear round the next bend.

Hastily she consulted the scrap of paper Coralie had thrust into her hand before she had left London. Yes, this must be the place, she decided, enquiring her way to Beck Cottage from an elderly man who had stopped on the pavement. He was out walking his dog and seemed eager to be of assistance.

'Beck Cottage?' he reflected. 'Let me see. That will be Miss Edgar's place. You'll go straight through the village and turn right along the beck—the river,' he explained in case she might have difficulty with the local term. 'It isn't far and you really can't go wrong.' He looked beyond her and Sandy smiled at him. 'You like dogs, young man?' he said, observing a small boy's interest in his pet. 'There are plenty of them hereabouts.'

Katherine thanked him as she pressed in her clutch.

'Not long now, Sandy,' she said. 'I expect you're hungry again!'

She found Beck Cottage at the very end of the lane, fronted by a busy little stream which hurried along between green banks scattered with opening daffodils. Someone had planted them a long time ago and they had multiplied to dress the river in gold as it flowed over its pebbly bed chuckling with its own importance. Four ducks swam downstream and a collection of hens picked their erratic way from behind the cottage on to the narrow road.

The cottage itself stood slightly aloof, its green storm doors securely closed against intrusion, its windows screened by white net curtains gathered closely against the panes. As Katherine rang the bell it looked anything but welcoming.

Sandy had tumbled out of the car behind her and stood waiting as she rang the bell for a second time.

'There's nobody in,' he remarked plaintively after a moment or two. 'They've all gone away.'

'It's all right,' Katherine assured him, aware that the remark had been a reflection of his general insecurity. 'Somebody must be here.'

The fact that she was not so sure of her own reaction dawned on her as the minutes fled away and they were still left standing there. The cottage looked closed, not just for the day but for some considerable time, although the four ducks and the hens were making their noisy way across the grass. Someone would surely return to feed them—Aunt Hattie full of apologies, no doubt, for offering her young nephew such a tardy welcome.

A woman in an apron made her appearance at the door of the cottage farther down the lane, hobbling towards them in her carpet slippers.

'Are you looking for Miss Edgar?' she asked, eyeing

them with frank curiosity. 'She be away to Austria for a month.'

'Austria?' Katherine echoed as if she had said Australia.

'Ay. She allus takes a holiday this time o' the year, an' this time it's Austria.'

'But she knew we were coming,' Katherine protested, before she remembered that it was only twenty-four hours since she had met Coralie at the party and taken on the responsibility of the child by her side who seemed more interested in four ducks than the fact that they were virtually stranded for the night.

'She didn't say nothink about you comin',' the woman informed her. 'Just asked me to feed the hens, as she allus does, an' look after old Rick. That's her dog. He's fast asleep at my kitchen fire; doesn't stir much when Miss Edgar be away, like. Doesn't get out much, an' that's all right by me since my feet be so bad I can't walk much!'

Katherine had to think quickly.

'I don't suppose you know when Miss Edgar will be back?' she asked, wondering for the first time where they were going to sleep.

'A month, she said, an' she stopped her papers and milk before she went. She be gone a week now. I get my own papers from the village. Tom Fender brings them when he's up wi' the car,' the woman advised her. 'Were you thinkin' of stayin' at the cottage?' she enquired inquisitively.

'It was what we expected to do.' Katherine thrust her fingers through her hair in a gesture she had when she came face to face with a tricky problem. 'I suppose there's somewhere in the village where we could stay.'

'I haven't the room,' the woman told her. 'There's Tom, you see. He's my lodger an' me an' my old man has the other bedroom. You could try at the pub, though. They take in summer guests an' you'd be comfortable enough there.'

Katherine nodded. She had passed the small hostelry

on her way through the village noticing that it seemed clean and was well looked after, like most Lakeland public houses.

'We'll go back there,' she decided.

'Can I say who called?' the woman asked, not to be done out of what would prove to be an evening's conversation when the lodger and her husband finally came in.

'It doesn't matter.' Katherine felt a sudden deep concern for her young charge. 'Miss Edgar wouldn't know who I was.'

'The wee lad's been here before,' the woman observed.

'Yes, I believe so.' Sudden anger flared in Katherine's heart. 'He must have come with his mother. He's Miss Edgar's nephew.'

'He was always runnin' after the hens,' the woman reminisced, 'but that was a year ago an' he's bigger now.' She smiled at Sandy, who offered her a tentative smile in return.

'I'm hungry,' he announced hopefully, blue eyes raised to the inquisitive brown ones.

'You'll be all right at the pub,' the woman said to Katherine.

The first thing she had to do was to get settled somewhere for the night. Katherine looked at her watch, seeing that it was almost seven o'clock. Supposing the pub refused to take such a late booking?

Driving quickly back down the road, she pulled up at the main door.

'Come on, Sandy,' she prompted, 'we've got to find a bed for the night.'

Their plight was obvious. One tired and hungry small boy and a girl on her own would surely touch the heart of even the most insensitive landlord.

The small entrance lobby was deserted, but there was a bell to ring on the counter over which hung the sign 'Reception' and it produced the desired result within minutes.

'Can I help you?'

A tall, fair-haired young woman in a blue jersey and kilted skirt had made her appearance at the inner doorway.

'I hope so,' said Katherine. 'I know it's very late, but we need accommodation. We expected to stay at Beck Cottage with Miss Edgar.'

'She's away.' The girl flicked over a page of the ledger on the counter. 'I can give you a double room with a small bed in it,' she decided obligingly. 'The wee lad looks tired.'

'And hungry!' Katherine said with relief. 'I'm sorry to have left it so late.'

'That's all right,' the girl smiled. 'We're not too busy at this time of year, between Easter and Whit, and we generally have a room to spare.' Sandy's fair head reached just above the counter. 'Will you take your meal together?' she asked. 'It would be a help not having to cook twice. There's only one other guest and he likes to dine early.'

Katherine felt as tired as Sandy looked and she was also conscious of a mounting anger when she thought about Coralie who had placed them carelessly in this predicament. It was quite obvious that her former school friend hadn't contacted her sister at Beck Cottage before she had sent them off on this wild goose chase, but by now she would surely know what had happened.

When she phoned Coralie from the comfortable bedroom under the eaves there was no reply. Even Coralie's flatmate appeared to be out. Drawing a swift breath, she took Sandy down to supper.

Apart from the elderly fisherman who occupied a table at the window, they were alone in the dining-room. As the receptionist had pointed out, it was a slack time of the year, yet subconsciously she seemed to be waiting for someone else to appear. All that Coralie had told her about Sandy's father came crowding into her mind, the fact that he was quite capable of a kidnap attempt where his son was concerned and the possibility of them being followed remaining uppermost in her thoughts as they ate the substantial meal which was set before them. It was such a satisfying meal that she was almost as sleepy as Sandy when it was over.

'Perhaps you'd like to have your coffee after you've put your little boy to bed?' the waitress suggested. 'I'm in sole charge tonight, but it wouldn't be any trouble. I generally have a cup myself around nine o'clock.'

When Sandy finally dropped off to sleep Katherine phoned London again, but there was still no answer. Wondering what she had expected Coralie to do about their predicament, she sat in the small, comfortable snug with her pot of coffee till ten o'clock, trying not to fall asleep before she phoned for the third time.

Going through the hall to the telephone box she had to pass the open door to the public bar where the hum of conversation and ready laughter only seemed to emphasise her own isolation. Through the glass screen she could see the locals gathered round the half moon of the counter or grouped around the marble-topped tables with pints of beer in their hands, but there was nobody there she recognised, although she was now thinking of Charles Moreton as her pursuer.

It was ridiculous, of course, a mad impulse arising out of the fact that he had sought her out at the party they had attended the evening before and been more or less determined to see her home afterwards. The point was that he had told her so little about himself, even though he had kissed her goodnight on the doorstep, a kiss which she still remembered. It had been brief and not at all demanding, as if he thought the gesture was expected of him in the circumstances as a matter of course, but it had left its mark. She would have thought that a man of Charles Moreton's calibre wouldn't kiss indiscriminately unless he had some good reason for the challenge.

Remembering that he had added almost casually, 'We'll meet again, would you say?' seemed to suggest that he wanted to renew their acquaintance some time in the future, but he had not made any definite rendezvous. He had asked a few pointed questions about her holiday, but that was all, and apart from his name he had told her nothing about himself.

Somewhere at the back of her mind she felt that he might have some connection with Coralie, a discarded suitor, maybe, wishing to know her whereabouts, but that didn't seem to fit the bill when her first impression of the man had been one of cold indifference to a transient love affair.

She hardly expected an answer to her final phone call and she returned the receiver to its hook with a little angry snap. How could Coralie be so exasperating? How could she go off somewhere to amuse herself when she must surely know by now that there was nobody at Beck Cottage to take her child?

CHAPTER TWO

EARLY the following morning Katherine phoned London again, almost expecting to draw a blank. Even Coralie's flatmate had flown the nest, and she went down to breakfast with Sandy's hand in hers, wondering what she should do next.

To return to London might be one way of solving the problem, but again it might not. It could be a long, frustrating journey which could end in disappointment. Katherine stood at the foot of the stairs, looking at Sandy with a new kind of pity in her heart as the word abandoned stuck in her mind. How could anyone have acted like Coralie had done without feeling a grievous remorse? She was Sandy's mother and she had expressed her love for him, and she was also extremely intelligent, wanting to succeed in her chosen career because of him, but how could she have left him entirely in a stranger's care when she knew that her ex-husband was determined to claim him one way or another?

She left Sandy in the dining-room coping with the last of the toast and marmalade while she went back to the bedroom to re-pack their cases. The child's tartan holdall lay on the smaller of the two beds and she folded his one-piece pyjama suit into it before she went to the adjoining bathroom to pick up their toilet bags. Sandy's was a vivid blue covered with nursery-rhyme characters which he had named for her the night before as he dutifully brushed his teeth with the miniature toothbrush which Coralie had packed for him before he had left London, and the small brush looked oddly pathetic as she dropped it into the waterproof bag, but suddenly her eye caught the sewn-on name-tape on one corner. Sandy Moreton, she read as her blood froze.

Sandy Moreton? Charles Moreton's child. It was painfully obvious now, after all that Coralie had told her. He had been there at the party in Kensington hoping to track Coralie down, but he must have arrived as Coralie had left, or soon afterwards. No, Katherine remembered, it was while she had been speaking to Coralie that she had first noticed the tall man in the grey suit at the far side of the noisy room, but Coralie had left so quickly afterwards that he could conceivably have missed her in the crowd. When he realised that Coralie had escaped him he had crossed the room to her side.

It all seemed to fall into place as she remembered: the questions he had asked; his interest in her future movements; the offer to see her home and, above all, the suggestion of coldness in his manner which had baffled her at the time but which she had foolishly taken for a natural reserve. He had been assessing her with a clinical detachment which now seemed all too obvious, and she had told him all he wanted to know. When they had eventually reached her flat she had told him that she could not invite him in because she was tired, and he had suggested that she would be leaving for Scotland the following morning. She hadn't had the wit to contradict him nor, at that time, the inclination. He had bowled her over completely as no doubt he had intended to do, and she had fallen for the treatment like a romantic teenager.

Ramming the toilet bags into her case, she zipped up Sandy's holdall and walked to the head of the stairs; then suddenly she was running down the hall as if her life depended on reaching the dining-room before disaster struck. But Sandy was still seated at the table in the corner, counting prune stones on to his side plate.

Hastily she paid her bill, driving back to the cottage as quickly as she could, but the kindly neighbour could tell her nothing further about Hattie Edgar.

'I'll have to make a phone call,' she decided. 'I wonder if you'd keep an eye on Sandy till I get back?'

'Why, of course! He'll be safe enough here, helping me

to feed the hens,' the woman said.

'I won't be long,' Katherine explained to Sandy. 'I'll buy some sweets.'

'He'll be safe enough.' The words echoed in her ears as she set off down the lane towards the phone box.

It was to be her final effort to contact Coralie in London, and she really didn't hold out much hope of success, but rather than phoning from the hotel she had decided to wait for a while and use the public kiosk she had noticed on a corner of the village street opposite the post office. Acknowledging it as a last resort, she knew that she would have to make up her mind about the future as soon as she had made it.

Keeping the receiver to her ear for several minutes while the number rang out, she wondered why she should be trying so persistently to reunite Coralie with her child, and then she knew that only Sandy mattered. She would go to the end of the world to save him distress.

Automatically she replaced the receiver, picking up the returned coins from the receptacle under the slots with a heavy heart. What to do now?

Out of the corner of her eye she saw a parked car on the far side of the road, a grey car with an odd familiarity about it. Her breath caught in her throat as she opened the kiosk door, but the parked vehicle was empty. In no way could she be absolutely sure that it was the car which had turned off the motorway immediately behind her to follow them all the way to Keswick and beyond.

As she crossed the road in search of the sweets she had promised Sandy, her heart appeared to be beating suffocatingly close to her throat, and then she saw him. Charles Moreton was coming out of the post office, replacing his wallet in the inside pocket of his jacket with a look of concentration on his face which deepened as he recognised her.

'Imagine seeing you!' Katherine exclaimed, keeping her voice quite steady, although she imagined that he could easily hear her wildly-beating heart. 'Are you on holiday?'

'I'm on my way to Scotland,' he said, giving her a quick calculating glance which seemed to strip her of all pretence.

'So am I—more or less.'

How else was she to answer him, since he appeared to know much more about her than she suspected?

'I passed you yesterday,' he said, standing squarely between her and retreat. 'You had a child in the car with you.'

Katherine had an almost compulsive desire to prevaricate, to stand between them and Coralie largely for Sandy's sake, but finally she said:

'I'm taking him to Scotland.' She had made up her mind to do just that, she realised.

'You've come slightly out of your way,' Charles Moreton observed dryly.

'I—we were going to a cottage just along the road,' she confessed, 'but his aunt isn't there. She left for Austria a week ago, so——'

'You've decided to take him with you to Scotland.' His eyes were as cold as steel, his gaze as incisive as he looked down at her.

'It wasn't really my intention,' she defended herself, 'but I can hardly abandon a three-year-old child in a strange village, can I?'

'Surely,' he suggested, 'you made some kind of provision for this kind of emergency.'

'Not really.' Katherine was remembering how little time Coralie had given her to arrange anything. 'Coralie—my friend was quite sure her sister would be here.'

He looked about him.

'It's remote enough,' he acknowledged with a hardness she had come to recognise in him. 'Where have you parked your car?'

Katherine felt suddenly cold. Everything Coralie had told her about this determined man was probably true.

'At the cottage,' she said dismissively. 'And I really must go. I thought I would pick up some sweets for the journey.' She turned towards the confectioner's shop next to the post office. 'Goodbye,' she said. 'I can't leave Sandy for too long.'

He probably knew that she had recognised him as a potential enemy because she had ranged herself on the side of his former wife, but he no longer barred her way and she passed him without further explanation. She saw him loitering on the pavement outside the bow-fronted window of the confectioner's with its pebble-glass panes and the jangling bell which heralded her approach to the counter, and the sharp ping of the bell seemed to echo too loudly in the silence as she waited.

'Can I help you?'

She was jolted back to the present by the question to find herself confronted by the shopkeeper.

'Yes. Yes, thank you.' She cast an apprehensive glance at the waiting figure on the pavement outside. 'Is there another way out?' she found herself asking.

'There's the tea-room.' The woman behind the counter looked surprised by her question. 'You could go through there and out into Beck Street.'

Hastily Katherine purchased some home-made candy, going quickly through the door which led to the tiny tea-room with a definite fear in her heart and running most of the way back to the cottage in the lane. Supposing something had happened to Sandy in her absence? Supposing he had been spirited away? Kidnapped had been the ugly word Coralie had used. 'His father is trying to kidnap him,' she had said with conviction. He would be ready to go to any length to recover his son, and that was the undoubted impression Katherine had formed during the past ten minutes as she had faced Charles Moreton across the cobbled pavement of the village street. He was a man who would offer no quarter once he had established the fact that she was in the plot to frustrate his immediate plans to take possession of his child.

Her heart sank as she thought about him, of the way she had reacted to his obvious charm on so short an acquaintance and the unexpected kiss which had shaken her to the foundations of her being. He had been playing on her susceptibility, flagrantly planning to use her for his own ends for as long as he could. Coralie had said that he would be ready to go to any lengths to recapture his son.

Sympathy vibrated in her for a moment as she realised how much he probably loved his child, but he had broken the law—or was about to break it—by snatching Sandy away.

Why? Because he was determined to get his hands on a great deal of money, Coralie had declared; because Sandy was a considerable heir under his uncle's will.

If the accusation was difficult to believe that was just another proof of her own gullibility, she told herself, running towards Beck Cottage with the bag of candy in her hand. She had told herself a hundred times not to accept people at face value, and it was a kind of madness to think that Charles Moreton might have been different.

Beck Cottage bore the same deserted look, but she drew a deep breath of relief at the sight of Sandy riding astride the neighbour's gate with the ducks in attendance.

'You get right down from there!' she admonished, her voice sharp with relief. 'We're leaving right away.' She moved towards her parked car. 'You can say goodbye to the ducks.'

'Did you get the sweets?' Sandy came obediently towards her.

'Yes. Get in.' She put the striped candy bag into his hand. 'We'll say goodbye to Mrs Yates and be on our way.'

Trying to find some trace of Charles in Sandy's bright little face, she drove back down the lane towards the road, but the child was too like Coralie with his fair, curling hair and sweeping dark lashes half veiling the incredibly blue eyes to bear comparison with anyone else. There was nothing in Sandy's features to suggest that Charles might be his father, but resemblances were not always easy to establish and Charles had acted out the part of her pursuer. Even now, he might still be waiting for her outside the confectioner's shop.

The fact that he could still be there firmed her resolve to get away. Whoever Charles was, she must leave him behind as fast as she could because she couldn't afford complications while she had yet to make up her mind where to go, but one thing she was certain about was the fact that she must keep her promise to Coralie, for Sandy's sake.

The Carlisle bypass was the most obvious way north, but she decided to take a more roundabout route when she came to the next junction. Both signposts said Penrith, and she drove on to the narrower road through Matterdale and Caldbeck.

All the way along the lovely, hidden dale she was conscious of a mounting tension, looking for a following car, but the innocent switchback road stretched empty behind her, the mountains closing in companionably as she drove north, and her spirits lifted.

'We'll play a game,' she suggested. 'Blue cars again, like your anorak. Let's count blue cars going the other way.'

Not grey cars. Definitely blue ones!

It was several miles before they met the first car, parked outside an inn on the valley floor where a narrow blue lake reflected the stretch of cloud-free sky above their heads.

'We'll have something to eat here,' Katherine suggested.

The innkeeper was a jolly, talkative man.

'I don't suppose you get many people here at this time of year,' Katherine remarked when he had set coffee and orange juice on the table before them.

'Not many. You're only the second today, in fact.'

Katherine's heart lurched, because she had been thinking of Charles Moreton.

'Was it long ago?' she asked.

'About an hour. He didn't wait. That's odd,' he added, glancing through the window to where she had parked her car by the lakeside. 'He asked if a girl in a blue car had passed this way with a child.' He looked from Katherine's flushed face to Sandy, who was half-way through his glass of orange juice, vastly intrigued by the red straw which had been provided with it. 'He must have been searching for you.'

'Was he driving a grey car—a Rover?'

'He was that, and he seemed in a great hurry, but perhaps you'll meet up with him on the motorway.'

It was the last thing she wanted to do, because she was convinced that it was indeed Charles Moreton who had enquired about her. Katherine rose to her feet. No more stops at obvious hotels, she thought, since he had been astute enough to choose the less frequently used dale road in his pursuit of her. The fact that he had left ahead of her was a bonus which she felt immeasurably thankful for, but they could so easily meet up with him again at a hotel farther along the road.

'Could you let me have a few sandwiches?' she asked. 'Just something light to eat in the car. We'll be having a meal somewhere when we stop for the night. I'd also be obliged if you could let me have some milk.'

'For the little 'un? Why, of course you can.' The innkeeper was greatly impressed by Sandy. 'You look as if you've come away in a hurry,' he observed, 'but we do packed lunches for the climbers, so I can let you have a couple. Alice will get you the milk if you come round to the kitchen,' he added. 'And I'll find you a couple of plastic beakers.'

Katherine was grateful and soon they were on their way again. Full of orange juice and biscuits, Sandy fell asleep and she put him in the back seat for safety—or was it because, lying down with the travelling rug wrapped securely round him, he would be less obvious from a passing car?

They reached the Border without incident, keeping off the motorway and threading their way along the side roads through little towns and villages, going by the less obvious route through Annan and Dumfries towards the coast.

Katherine had consulted her road map before Dumfries, making her decision to keep to the west in her attempt to shake off a grey Rover which would surely have kept to the main way north.

Suddenly carefree, she looked about her at the bright panorama of the Kirkcudbright hills, at Corserine and Merrick with their heads in the clouds and the deep valley of the Doon opening up before her. Surely no one would think of following her along such an unlikely route.

Sandy stirred and they ate their sandwiches and hard-boiled eggs on a hilltop where they could look down on the loch.

'We'll stretch our legs,' she suggested, running down the hill as he followed her. 'It's like having wings, Sandy, isn't it, with all the wind behind us?'

The blue eyes sparkled.

'I've got a kite,' he said. 'I can fly it on the moor when we get to Glassary.'

It was the first time he had spoken of any sort of home environment, a brief reference to the past which had obviously no connection with a London flat, but Katherine thought that the memory of Glassary might disturb him and steered the conversation in another direction. No child, no matter how young, could fail to remain untouched by a broken marriage, and Sandy was a sensitive little boy who evidently remembered his former home. The fact that he had rarely mentioned Coralie also disturbed her, but boys often kept a stiff upper lip even at a tender age, and she decided to amuse Sandy without mentioning his mother.

When they set off in the car again she followed the course of the Doon to Ayr where they had their first glimpse of the sea. The vast, open Firth of Clyde sparkled in the spring sunshine, delighting Sandy, who gazed out across the blue water to the hills of Arran, pressing his nose close to the window to watch for boats.

It was his obvious fascination which made her think of the car ferry from Gourock which would take them across the estuary to Dunoon, but the ferry was pulling away from the pier as they rounded the point at the Cloch lighthouse and she knew that she would have an hour or more to wait for the next one. Better, she thought, to press on and put Loch Lomond behind her before she thought of somewhere to spend the night.

Wondering again about her final destination, she came to the conclusion that there was only one thing to do. She must go ahead with her own plans and take Sandy with her. His small tartan grip was in the boot of the car beside her own suitcase, packed for a lengthy stay with Miss Edgar, who was now in Austria, address unknown, so it was more or less inevitable that she should look after this child till she could eventually contact his mother, who had been so certain that he would be safely installed in Beck Cottage in a remote Lakeland village by now.

Once or twice during the next hour as she skirted Glasgow by using the Erskine Bridge to cross the river, she wondered if she had any real right to continue her journey in this way, but then she remembered Coralie and the blue eyes which were so like Sandy's and felt herself justified. She would carry on with her own plans to go to the Trossachs until she could contact Sandy's mother and ask Coralie to collect her son at a given rendezvous farther north.

Sandy was delighted with their flight across the bridge which rose in a high, slender arc above the narrowing Clyde, his large, sombre eyes taking in the strange atmosphere with interest.

'Will Mummy come?' he asked unexpectedly, gazing down at the grey river as they passed.

Taken by surprise, Katherine hesitated.

'Soon,' she promised. 'I'll phone her when we stop for

some tea, just to make sure.'

An odd reluctance to part with him had made her hesitate, but there really wasn't any room for sentiment at this stage, she tried to tell herself. Sandy wasn't hers, although how anyone could part with him as casually as Coralie had done was beyond her comprehension. The word Coralie had used about him was 'docile', but it wasn't quite true. At the tender age of three and a bit there was an odd sort of acceptance about Sandy which had already touched her heart.

By the time they had reached Loch Lomond he was asleep again and she was forced to make another decision—whether to go on or spend the night at Tarbet. Sandy was tired and so was she, but at least Sandy was able to sleep. She pressed on, reaching Ardlui as the sun dipped towards the western mountains and going into Glen Falloch in search of a suitable resting place for the night.

She had travelled that way before, but she had completely forgotten about its loneliness and the lack of amenities among some of Scotland's grandest mountains. The Trossachs had been her vague destination, but now she was to the west of them with the great bens and lochs of the Highlands ahead of her.

To go on, or veer to the west towards Oban and the Isles?

The car made her decision for her. The engine noise of which she had been vaguely aware since Ardlui became more pronounced, reaching a grinding crescendo as she pulled into the next passing-bay.

Sandy slept on in blissful ignorance of their plight, undisturbed by the fact that the soporific motion of the car had ceased, and Katherine decided not to waken him even to offer him one of the left-over sandwiches from their alfresco lunch.

Lifting the bonnet, she gazed at the engine, realising how little she knew about the mechanics of her hitherto reliable mode of travel, and finally coming to the conclusion that she was in need of professional help. Looking about her, she was quickly aware that she could not have been stranded in a more lonely place. She was well into the glen surrounded on every side by formidable mountains rearing their heads against the paling blue of the northern sky as they crowded the horizon, one above the other, rising over three thousand feet to the knees of Ben More. The great ben dominated everything, with Stob Binnein and Stob Garb and Cruach Ardrain crowding around the lesser giants of the Grampians to form a barrier to her further progress.

The suggestion of their invincible might dismayed her for a moment until she forced herself to think back. A little way along the road she had passed a telephone kiosk. It could not be more than half a mile away and it was her only means of dealing with her present situation. In over an hour she hadn't passed another car.

Tucking the travelling rug more securely around her sleeping passenger, she locked the back door and set out, but when she reached the kiosk it was out of order—vandalised. Not here, she thought. Surely not in a place like this!

The fact remained, however, that her one means of reaching the outside world had been denied her, and she hurried back to the lay-by. She had not passed one single vehicle in the time it had taken her to walk to the kiosk and run back.

Breathless, she opened the car door. Sandy had gone.

Seconds passed as she gazed incredulously at the empty back seat. Her travelling rug lay on the floor, the cushion which had cradled Sandy's head tossed aside as if to suggest that he had no further use for it, yet nothing else had been disturbed. She searched the boot, but both her own suitcase and his little tartan grip were still there.

'Sandy!' she called in her desperation. 'Where are you?'

It was a cry from the heart, she realised, a plea which she really didn't expect to be answered, and her mind seemed to go blank for a moment, but finally she told herself that a child of Sandy's age would hardly wander away from the security of a parked car even if the sun was still shining and only the great shadow of the bens darkened the glen.

She shivered as she looked about her at the stark beauty of the surrounding mountains which she would have appreciated so much under happier circumstances. There was no sound except for the gurgle of running water somewhere near at hand, nothing to suggest human habitation for the next few miles.

She listened, tensed, for the sound of another car, but all was quietness and peace. Peace in nature, but not in her own heart, she thought, knowing a sudden, panic fear. She had done the most foolish thing imaginable, leaving Sandy asleep in the car and locking the back door but not her own. It had been such a short distance to the kiosk, not much more than half a mile, but in the space of time it had taken her to reach the box and run back Sandy had disappeared.

Why had she felt impelled to run? Even before she had reached the lay-by there had been a sense of panic in her, the need to protect a little boy with curly fair hair and amazingly blue eyes who had put a small, trusting hand in her own and gone with her willingly into this absurd adventure.

Angry with herself and her mechanical ignorance, she explored the engine again, although with little real hope, her head under the bonnet as she checked water and oil, which was something she did know about. Then, shattering the silence, she heard the sound she had been waiting for. A car was approaching along the road ahead of her. Help was at hand.

Even before the Rover swung into the lay-by she knew who her rescuer must be.

'Having trouble?'

Charles Moreton had caught up with her.

'So it was you?' Katherine glared at him angrily. 'What have you done with him?' She searched the back of the grey car. 'You took Sandy, didn't you? You've—kidnapped him!'

Charles looked slightly amused.

'It's a strong word to use, but yes, I've taken him,' he agreed. 'If you're concerned about his safety, however, you needn't worry,' he added. 'He's in good hands.'

'Yours, I suppose you mean?' she challenged. 'But that isn't quite good enough. I promised to look after him, to—to protect him.'

'You weren't exactly doing that when you left him alone in a parked car with a door open,' he pointed out, the smile fading from his eyes.

Katherine took a step towards him.

'What have you done with him?' Her voice was not quite steady, although it was absurd to suppose that he had harmed his own child. 'Where have you taken him?'

'He's in safe keeping not more than a mile away.'

'I demand to know where!' She stamped her foot. 'You're not to be trusted.'

His eyes were ice-cold as he gazed back at her and there was a cruel twist to his mouth as he said:

'I suppose Coralie told you that.'

'She did, and I think it must be true. You've been following me for two days ever since we left London, and in the end you took Sandy without a word.'

The hard mouth looked even harder as he continued to gaze at her.

'Has it never occurred to you that you might be equally suspect where I'm concerned?' he asked. 'Up until two days ago we'd never met, and then I discover you're aiding and abetting Coralie in one of her wilder schemes.'

'I was helping her to protect her child,' Katherine cried defensively. 'There can be no harm in that when she was at her wits' end, not knowing what to do.'

'You're painting me a picture of a Coralie I've never seen,' he assured her cynically. 'How well do you really know her?'

'Well enough to imagine how she must feel,' Katherine

declared. 'I know how much she must hate the idea of parting with her child.'

'Where is she now?' he demanded as if he hadn't heard her defence of Sandy's mother.

'I don't know.' It was a lame sort of admission even if it was the truth.

'You can't hope to protect her by lying.' He took her by the arm, his fingers sinking into her flesh as he sought to detain her.

'I'm not lying!' Katherine cried. 'I phoned her from the Lake District last night and again this morning——'

'And?' he prompted, still holding her.

'There was no reply.'

'That hardly surprises me,' he said dryly.

She shook herself free.

'I'm not going to discuss Coralie,' she declared, 'but I think I sympathise with her now, more than ever. You're completely ruthless,' she accused. 'The man in authority, no doubt, in your own environment, but you have no right to take Sandy under the circumstances.'

'I think I have every right.' He moved towards the back of the car. 'If you'll give me your keys I'll get Sandy's bag.'

She rubbed her arm where she could still feel the grip of his strong fingers.

'No,' she said firmly. 'I'm not handing him over like this as if he were some kind of chattel. I agree I was foolish,' she rushed on, 'leaving him alone even for so short a time, but he was fast asleep and I knew I hadn't far to go to reach the phone box.'

'Did it not occur to you that he might have wakened up and been afraid?' he asked icily.

'I thought of that, but it was the chance I had to take,' she admitted.

'You appear to take chances easily,' Charles Moreton pointed out.

'Not as a rule.'

'But this time,' he suggested with deepening sarcasm,

'you couldn't resist helping an old school friend? I find that touching in the extreme.'

He held out his hand, but she kept the keys.

'I don't intend you to get away with this,' she decided. 'I'm not going to hand over Sandy's luggage just because you say so. He's my responsibility at present.'

'And mine.' A flash of anger sparked in the grey eyes under the beetling black brows. 'Please let me have your keys.'

He continued to hold out his hand, his angry gaze transfixing her, and foolishly Katherine put the keys on top of the boot. A physical struggle with this man was out of the question, she told herself.

'Thank you!'

He opened the boot, taking out Sandy's gay tartan grip and, surprisingly, her own suitcase, laying them aside on the road.

'The case is mine,' she pointed out.

'I gathered that.' He picked up both case and bag. 'Have you a coat in the car?'

'Yes.' She answered him confusedly. 'But what has that to do with all this?' she demanded.

'You're coming with me. Obviously your car has broken down and I've told you Sandy is safely installed for the night not too far away.' He looked at her with a gleam of derision in his eyes. 'Surely you don't expect me to leave you where you are in the circumstances? You needn't worry about your car,' he added. 'I'll send someone to look at it in the morning.'

'You're very kind.' There was a suggestion of sarcasm in her own voice now. 'If it wasn't for Sandy I'd refuse, but I don't mean to lose track of him so easily.'

Charles walked towards the Rover.

'Make sure you lock up properly this time,' he advised.

Katherine got into the parked Rover because it was the only thing she could do. Her heart was beating strongly as she took her seat beside her captor, belying her outward calm which she wanted him to recognise as determination.

'I don't intend to let Sandy go,' she said belligerently.

'I wouldn't expect you to.' His tone was cold. 'You had a great deal of courage to come this far after your experience at Beck Cottage. You must have known you were on a wild goose chase by then.'

'I wasn't chasing anyone!' Katherine declared. 'It was you who was doing the following bit, like some shabby private eye!'

He evidently found that amusing, because he laughed outright.

'What are you trying to say?' he demanded. 'That you have every right to Sandy and I have none?'

'Coralie has more right than either of us,' Katherine reminded him. 'She is Sandy's mother.'

His mouth tightened again and she found herself looking at him in profile as he drove on without answering her. There was something about the high, arched nose and dark, beetling brows which disconcerted her now, suggesting a bird of prey, although she had formerly admired them in London, and certainly Coralie had used similar words to describe him before they had parted. 'My ex-husband wants Sandy because he's the heir to a great deal of money,' she had said agitatedly. 'His uncle settled a considerable sum on him when he was one year old and my ex is determined to have full control of it.'

They motored on with long silences developing between them, although Katherine's mind was actively at work. She did not trust this man now that she knew more about him. She had been primed to resent him, but she could not fail to recognise his strength.

'Where are you taking me?' she was forced to ask at last.

'To Sandy. I thought that might be obvious,' he answered. 'He's quite safe, I assure you, but I think you should remain with him till he's completely settled in. He seems to have become quite attached to you.'

'Settled in?' she repeated. 'And where might that be?

You have no right to take the law into your own hands,' she rushed on. 'This is a—a double kidnapping!'

He smiled at the suggestion.

'Believe me,' he said, 'it's highly coincidental. You're hardly a child, and when I have no further use for your services I'll let you go. It's quite obvious that Sandy trusts you and I have to protect him from the shock of too many strangers.'

'But you don't hesitate when it comes to the trauma of separating him from his mother, which is a child's natural protection,' she declared angrily.

'No.' The square, determined jaw was firmly set, the steely eyes cold. 'You promised to look after Sandy and I mean to hold you to your word.'

Within an hour they had reached their destination. Turning the car off the road through the glen, Charles crossed a main highway to run along a wide strath where high peaks looked down on them in the gathering dusk, grim mountains crowding in on them from the north and east to make an easy prison from which it would be hard to escape.

Without the help of her road map Katherine felt completely lost, yet when they finally pulled up at the hotel their welcome could not have been warmer.

The proprietress came out to shake her companion by the hand, calling him by his Christian name.

'I'm sorry I wasn't here when you first arrived, Chay,' she apologised, 'but everything is arranged.'

She was a small, stout woman in her early fifties, amazingly reassuring in a well-fitting tweed skirt and matching cashmere jersey, and her curiosity when she looked at Katherine seemed only natural.

'My name's Katherine Rivers,' Katherine offered swiftly. 'I'm looking after Sandy.'

A quick glance passed between the proprietress and her captor.

'I thought Callum could pick up Miss Rivers' car and take it into Killin in the morning,' Charles Moreton said.

'I hadn't time to look at it.'

The small, dark woman held out her hand.

'You've had quite an adventure, I understand,' she remarked guardedly. 'You must be ready for a wash and something to eat.' She turned back to Charles. 'I've put the wee one to his bed,' she explained. 'He was tired and fair bewildered by all that travelling when Callum brought him in. It was lucky you met him on the road and he could bring Sandy here while you went back to look at the car.'

So that was how Sandy had travelled so far in the meantime, Katherine thought. Charles had met a friend on his way to the hotel and passed Sandy on to him while he turned back to the lay-by in search of her. He had all the luck!

'Thanks, Morag,' Charles was saying. 'I knew you would help all you could.'

'Why not?' Morag's dark eyes searched his face. 'If there's anything else I can do you have only to say the word.'

'I know that,' Charles agreed, 'but we'll go on in the morning, I think. I want to get back to the Lodge as quickly as possible.'

To my ultimate prison, Katherine thought dramatically. But surely this sort of thing couldn't happen in this day and age?

Charles Moreton's attitude to their hostess was completely relaxed, and they were evidently on the friendliest of terms as they spoke about local matters standing in the low, raftered entrance hall for several minutes before they ascended the stairs. It would be hopeless to appeal to Morag, Katherine thought, while she so openly trusted Charles and was so eager to help him.

'May I see Sandy?' she asked at the top of the narrow staircase.

Another quick glance passed between her hostess and Charles Moreton.

'He's sound asleep,' said Morag as if at some unspoken

command. 'It would be a pity to disturb him. You're near enough,' she added. 'I've put you in the room next door.'

And where would Charles Moreton sleep? Somewhere not too far away along the same corridor, Katherine imagined, a grim guardian between her and the stairs.

As soon as she was left alone in the small single room which was more than adequate for her needs she opened the door, making sure that the corridor was empty before she moved silently towards the door on her left. It was ajar and she pushed it open, to be immediately confronted by a pair of questioning grey eyes.

'Were you looking for me?' Charles Moreton enquired with a faint smile. 'Or was it just for the quickest way of escape?'

'Neither.' Her cheeks were pink with embarrassment and a vague anger. 'I was looking for Sandy's room.'

'To make sure I hadn't spirited him away again?' he queried. 'Why are you so suspicious of my intentions, Miss Rivers? I told you he was safe enough.' He came across the room to stand looking down at her. 'We don't exactly trust each other,' he concluded, 'and that's quite natural under the circumstances, wouldn't you say? How long have you really known Coralie?' he demanded.

'I told you we were at school together, but it was some time ago. Over six years ago, in fact. We met again at Millie Downhill's party.'

'Do you really expect me to believe that?' he asked coldly. 'When I noticed you it seemed that you were the best of friends.'

'I don't care what you thought,' said Katherine. 'I'm telling you the truth. I was coming north next day and I promised to take Sandy to his aunt in the Lake District.'

'Because I was about to snatch him,' he suggested. 'I suppose that was what Coralie told you.'

'Well, weren't you?' Her voice was suddenly harsh.

'Not without discussing it,' he declared. 'I went to Millie's party because I knew she would be there and she had been refusing to see me. She left rather hurriedly, you have to admit.'

'She'd gone to meet someone—a business contact, I think—only he didn't turn up and she felt she was wasting her time.'

'But she hadn't,' he said carefully. 'She'd met you and you'd promised to smuggle Sandy out of London early in the morning before anyone noticed.'

'You did!' she said. 'You must have seen me leave my flat with Sandy in the car. Perhaps that was why you asked to see me home from Kensington the night before. It wasn't really because it was raining and I might get wet, was it? It wasn't even because you were—attracted by me as a person,' she rushed on, remembering that disturbing kiss. 'It was because you wanted to know where I lived so that you could check on my movements.' The memory of the kiss he had pressed against her lips as a matter of course wouldn't go away, the goodnight kiss he had imagined she would expect, and a bright colour flooded her cheeks. 'You thought I was the kind of person you could cheat easily,' she accused him, 'fair game in your plot to take Sandy away from his mother, but you'll find I'm not. I won't stand idly by and allow you to kidnap him!'

Charles held the door wide open.

'To prove that my intentions are not as diabolical as you think they are,' he said smoothly, 'we'll look in on Sandy now, but don't forget he's a very tired little boy you've driven over three hundred miles with hardly a stop in order to avoid me. He needs his sleep.'

'How did you find my car?' she asked, hesitating on the threshold of Sandy's room.

'It was an amazing stroke of luck,' Charles admitted. 'I lost you just north of Bassenthwaite because I was ahead of you. I had a fair idea you'd chose the Caldbeck road because it was the less obvious one, but I thought you'd gone straight off from the confectioner's. Instead, I suppose you went back to the cottage for Sandy, and I should have thought of that. When I didn't catch up with you I rejoined the motorway, which was my second mistake, though it did get me here ahead of you.'

'You had no idea where I was going,' she protested. 'How did you feel so sure I would choose the Trossachs?'

'Because you talked about them at the party and I took a chance when I discovered that Aunt Hattie was no longer available,' he said.

'I came by the west coast after Carlisle,' Katherine admitted, 'by Erskine Bridge and Loch Lomond, but I could quite easily have branched off to Oban—or anywhere else,' she pointed out.

'My luck was in,' he said. 'I felt it might be. There are very few roads—main roads, anyway—in this part of the Highlands which you could have taken, and I didn't think you would stray into the byways. When you weren't here, at the hotel, as I fancied you might be, I set out to look for you. It was still a chance in a million that I found you—or rather, Sandy.'

'Abandoned?' she said harshly. 'But you must have known I'd be at my wits' end when I got back to the car and found him missing.'

'I'm afraid I didn't think about that,' he said coldly. 'Not too much, anyway. I made my decision quickly because he'd wakened up, but I suppose I'd made up my mind from the beginning not to let you go quite so easily so that you could contact Coralie again.'

Katherine stepped across the threshold of Sandy's room without answering him and he allowed her a brief glimpse of a tired little boy with chubby arms flung out across a flowered quilt and his clothes neatly folded on a nearby chair.

'Touching, isn't it?' he queried.

She turned away.

'I don't know how you can speak so casually when you're determined to take him away from Coralie. She's his mother.'

'Coralie appears to forget that when it suits her,' he

said grimly, closing the door on the sleeping child. 'When you've had a wash and change there'll be a meal waiting for you downstairs,' he added. 'Morag and her daughter are old friends of mine.'

'Staunch allies, I suppose you mean!'

'If you like,' he agreed. 'They would never let me down.'

Someone had carried her suitcase up to the adjoining room, but her car keys had not been returned. Impulsively she thought to ring and ask for them, and then she knew that they would still be in Charles Moreton's possession. It was as effective a way as any to keep her prisoner.

Running a bath, she watched the brown spring water gushing from the taps, finding it soft and caressing to the touch as she stepped in. A shower wouldn't have been quite so comforting at the ending of such a stressful day, she thought, luxuriating deliberately in this unexpected luxury in such a remote place, but eventually she had to step out and towel herself dry. There were movements in the next room, a rush of water as a shower was turned on, and the banging of a door as someone went downstairs. Charles, no doubt, in a hurry to brief his friends again before she reached the dining-room.

Almost reluctantly she left her own room, pausing for a moment at Sandy's door to listen, but there was no sound from within. Sleep had taken over inevitably, and if she had driven too far and too quickly in one day she was quite sure that Sandy would rise refreshed in the morning. He was a sturdy little boy who would cope well enough with a couple of days' motoring.

Two days, she thought, almost unable to believe that it was so short a time since she had met Charles Moreton for the first time and allowed him to escort her home from Millie Downhill's party. It seemed, even now, that he had been in her life for a very long time.

The friendly welcome of a log fire met her when she reached the foot of the stairs. It was almost dark now, but the lights in the hall had not been lit and it was only as she approached the fireplace that she was aware of someone sitting there. A tall girl in a woollen dress the colour of spent heather rose to her feet, the firelight picking out the glow of her magnificent red hair as she held out her hand.

'I'm Emma Falkland,' she introduced herself. 'Chay and I are lifelong friends.' For a moment a guarded hostility masked her candid hazel eyes. 'I live here,' she added. 'I'm "poor Emma" who never quite made it anywhere else.' The admission was ruefully amused. 'I help my mother to run the hotel, but perhaps Chay has already told you that?'

'No.' Katherine moved nearer to the hearth into the circle of firelight where she could study Emma Falkland to better advantage. 'He hasn't told me very much, as perhaps you know,' she said.

It was no use pretending that she had come here willingly as Charles Moreton's guest, she thought, for these were his acknowledged friends who would know all there was to know about Sandy and Coralie and perhaps about her own part in this strange adventure. They would have prejudged her as Coralie's friend and would be ready to treat her as a potential enemy.

'I know that Chay's terribly worried about Sandy,' Emma Falkland informed her almost aggressively, 'and I can't imagine what you hope to gain by all this. Surely you can't expect to win when you have Chay to contend with,' she added. 'He's the most ruthless man I know when he believes himself justified—the complete adversary. Having said that, I suppose I should wish you luck.' She continued to study Katherine. 'How long have you known Sandy's mother?' she demanded.

'We went to school together.' Katherine was tired of so much explanation. 'She was slightly older than I was and I suppose I looked up to her from a distance, as schoolgirls do.'

'And now?' Emma demanded sharply.

'We met at a party in London a few days ago.'

Emma's eyebrows shot up in genuine surprise.

'As recently as that?' she said. 'The infatuation must have been complete!'

Katherine's steady gaze held hers.

'You can call it fascination if you like—even a schoolgirl crush—but I felt compelled to help Coralie when I saw how distressed she was. Wouldn't you have done the same?'

Emma hesitated.

'I may not be so easily taken in,' she said, switching on the wall lights as Charles appeared at the outer door.

'You still have my car keys,' Katherine reminded him. 'May I have them back, please?'

'They'll be needed in the morning,' he told her. 'I've been to look at your car, but I can't do anything. Someone will take it to the garage in the morning. Hullo, Emma!' he added, giving the older girl a warm, if not to say affectionate smile. 'How's the latest sculpture coming along?'

'Not too well.' Emma seemed to be avoiding his direct gaze. 'I've had other things to think about these past few weeks.'

'Of course.' He turned back to Katherine. 'Emma is our local artist,' he explained. 'She fashions marvellous little animals out of wood and stone which Sandy finds irresistible, but we're finding it difficult to persuade her to make a proper career of it at present.'

'How can I do that when I'm mostly up to my elbows in flour and baking powder?' Emma demanded. 'Besides, I like being here. "Making a proper career" would mean branching out, going to Edinburgh or London where I would be recognised if I was good enough.'

'But you are good enough,' Charles said with conviction. 'You have a considerable talent which you're hiding under the proverbial bushel at present.'

'Chay, don't exaggerate!' Emma's protest was accompanied by an affectionate smile. 'You know that what I do is quite ordinary and I do it largely to please myself. It's a grand hobby, making the days pass more quickly, and in the summer months I get to know the tourists who come to the studio to watch. And buy!' she added with a touch of modest pride.

'You don't take yourself seriously enough,' said Charles, but somehow Katherine knew that he didn't believe that. Emma was very serious indeed.

Morag Falkland came through from the kitchen to announce that their meal was ready.

'Emma has set it in the snug,' she said. 'We're only family tonight.'

The intimate meal in the small room off the dining-hall was something Katherine hadn't expected. Seated between Charles and her hostess with the watchful Emma facing them, it was difficult to relax, although Morag Falkland seemed to be friendly enough. She was a cheerful little woman who had news of everyone for miles around which she dispensed for Charles's benefit, pausing occasionally to sketch in a background here and there for her guest.

'Everybody knows everyone else in these parts,' she explained. 'We're a scattered community, but we keep in touch. Distance is no object when we visit, for instance, and when anyone is going to Perth or Oban they generally set out with a formidable list of shopping to do. It has been known for the odd ram to be brought back in the back of a Range Rover, or a freezer or even a suite of furniture!'

It was general information, Katherine realised, with nothing personal to distinguish it from the ordinary run-of-the-mill conversation which could have been expected in a wayside inn, yet underneath it was the suggestion of reserve, a caution which must be largely due to her own presence among them.

Charles was a little more relaxed in his friends' company, she noticed, probably because he was now master of the situation, but he, too, kept the conversation general as the meal progressed.

'We're not quite as isolated as you might think,' he told

her as Morag produced a plate of home-baked oatcakes to eat with their cheese, 'and we're busy enough not to worry about it.'

'Sandy spoke of a place called Glassary,' Katherine remembered.

'As I see it, Glassary is Sandy's home,' he returned grimly. 'We'll be going out there in the morning.'

It had all been taken care of, planned, no doubt, even before he had left for London in search of his son. Katherine looked across the table at Emma Falkland, wondering what part she had to play in the drama of Glassary, but Emma was busy with their empty plates, gathering them on to a tray to be carried into the kitchen when the meal was finished.

'We'll have our coffee by the fire,' said Morag, rising to lead the way. 'The Forestry boys will be in later on and then there'll be no more privacy! It's early yet for visitors,' she turned to Katherine to explain, 'but we're the nearest rendezvous for the Forestry settlement in the glen. They come for darts and the odd dance from time to time, but there's nothing special this week. Just the usual high spirits plus an argument or two!'

'Do you mind if I go to bed early?' Katherine was genuinely tired now. 'If we're leaving again in the morning——'

'There won't be any particular hurry,' Charles assured her. 'We're almost at Glassary.'

Wondering why he hadn't gone straight to their destination instead of coming to the hotel, she supposed that 'almost' could mean anything up to another fifty miles or even more, and he had been genuinely concerned about Sandy's fatigue. When the first of the Forestry workers made their appearance she drank what was left of her coffee with undue haste, rising to go. Escape, she thought, might be the better word. Charles crossed to her side.

'Had enough for one day?' he enquired casually. 'It's going to be noisy down here for a while, but you won't hear it in your room. The walls are very thick.'

Like the walls at Glassary, she thought; prison walls, shutting out sound.

'How far is Glassary?' she asked.

'Less than thirty miles. There's no need for you to feel lost. I'll find you a map in the morning,' he offered.

'It sounds remote,' she suggested.

'Not too remote. It's a sizeable house with a village settlement at the head of the glen.'

'Your own particular kingdom!' she observed dryly.

'More or less.' He looked satisfied with the suggestion. 'I take a certain pride in it, though part of my time I have to work elsewhere.'

'In London, for instance?'

'Edinburgh is nearer home. I'm an accountant, but Glassary has always been my first love, quite apart from being a splendid investment. I run sheep in the glen and breed cattle to please myself.'

'And that's why you want Sandy so much,' she concluded. 'You need the satisfaction of knowing Glassary will always bear your name, that you have an heir to inherit all you've built.'

'I don't think I've looked so far into the future,' he said, opening the door for her.

The hall was rapidly filling with big, tough-looking men, most of them in hand-knitted Aran sweaters and rubber boots up to their knees, looking as if they had just come off the hill. A few had made a concession to convention by donning shirts and a tie, but most of them were heavily bearded and didn't seem to think them necessary. They were quiet men, ready to relax after a long day in the open, and they regarded her with surprise.

Charles was quite well known to them, but they treated him with obvious respect, although they used his Christian name.

'Your friends?' Katherine suggested.

'I'm glad to say.' He walked with her to the stairs. 'We need that sort of contact up here, and you know about friendship, I think.'

It was an oblique reference to why she was in her present situation, she realised, remembering how he had asked what she was prepared to give to her own friendship. 'Are you an obliging friend, Kate?' he had asked when they had first met, and perhaps that was what he was thinking about now.

'Goodnight,' she said. 'I hope someone will waken me in the morning.'

'In case I go off with Sandy without letting you know?' he queried with a sardonic smile. 'I have no intention of doing that. Sleep well, Kate!'

He had used her Christian name with a new kind of caution, but she knew that he could not be offering an olive branch. He was still suspicious of her actions in taking Sandy from London, still angry and possibly seeking revenge.

CHAPTER THREE

IN the morning she rose early enough, but someone was up before her. She opened her window to a clatter of pails in the paved area below and the sound of hens clucking as they gathered round the back door. The air she breathed in was cool and sweet, coming straight from the hills with a hint of pine in it, and she saw the trees marching in their neat ranks up to the skyline, clothing the once barren moorland with lush green and the paler fronds of larch.

It was a magic world to discover after a restless night in which she had dreamed of pursuing Sandy and Coralie to the edge of a cliff where she inevitably lost them.

Shivering a little, she washed in ice-cold spring water which had come straight off the hill without the benefit of passing through an inadequate heating system, thinking that it was obviously too early in the day to expect the luxury of hot water and that it didn't matter, anyway. It was no more than seven o'clock.

As she dressed she listened for the sound of movement in the adjoining rooms, but the walls were thick, as Charles had observed. Yet small children were often noisy when they first woke up in the joyous anticipation of a new day, and she wondered if Sandy had really been spirited away to Glassary in spite of Charles Moreton's promise.

Finishing her dressing in haste, she pulled open her bedroom door and hurried towards Sandy's room.

'Are we awake?' she asked before she saw that the bed was empty.

The curtains had been drawn back to their fullest extent, letting in the morning sun, but Sandy and his small tartan holdall were nowhere to be seen. Katherine ran to the window to look out. The hens were gathered in a squabbling clutch around some scattered corn, but the yard itself was deserted. Her heart seemed to miss a beat. They've gone, she thought. Charles has taken Sandy and doublecrossed me!

When he had discussed Glassary so freely the evening before it had all been a tremendous bluff. A vague disappointment struggled with the anger she felt as she hurried down the stairs to the hall below. Someone had cleared up the debris of the evening before and the sound of voices came from the snug, Sandy's high-pitched treble and a deeper masculine voice which she realised with a surge of relief belonged to Charles.

She found them both seated at the table supping porridge from white, blue-banded bowls.

'You must have been up very early,' she remarked, trying to keep the sound of relief out of her voice.

'Sandy had to feed the hens.' Charles rose to his feet. 'Do you take porridge?' he asked formally.

'I will this morning,' she agreed. 'I suppose it's the change of air that makes one feel so hungry.'

'After London,' he said, ringing the bell on the wall by the fireplace, 'fresh air and an appetite comes as a surprise.'

Katherine looked at her watch.

'I thought I might be up before anyone else,' she said.

'It's quarter to eight.' He pulled out a chair for her. 'I'm going to take another look at your car—and don't put sugar on your porridge!' he warned in a tone he hadn't used before.

Sandy greeted her thoughtfully.

'This is the way you take it,' he said, dipping his spoonful of porridge into the small side bowl next to his plate. 'It's——' He hesitated before a word he had heard often enough. 'Trinishinal,' he declared on a note of triumph.

'I must remember to be traditional!' Katherine laughed, sitting down beside him. 'You'll have to show me how at first, because it seems I've been away from Scotland for far too long!'

A young girl in a flowered pinafore came in with fresh porridge.

'That's Kirsty,' Sandy announced, spoon pointing. 'She helped me to feed the hens.'

'So I did,' Kirsty beamed a shy smile in his direction. 'And now you've eaten all your porridge you can have an egg.'

Sandy laid his spoon in his empty bowl.

'Will I drink the rest of the cream?' he asked obligingly.

'As much as you like!' Kirsty laughed. 'I'll bring some more.'

Sandy looked up from his bowl as Emma Falkland came in. She had evidently had her breakfast and no doubt she had tidied up in the lounge after she had finished.

'I'm going down to the studio,' she said after she had greeted Katherine with a brief nod. 'Would you like to come?'

Sandy was on his feet in an instant, taking her hand, and Katherine was quick to recognise the affinity which existed between them.

'What about that egg?' she asked. 'Kirsty was going to bring you one.'

'I'll wait till you finish,' Emma promised, sitting down on the window-seat. 'Did you sleep well, Miss Rivers?' she asked.

'Very well, and I thought I was up first this morning, but evidently I was last!' Katherine wanted to be friendly. 'Can I come to the studio, too?'

Emma looked surprised.

'There's nothing much to see.' She hesitated. 'Come if you like.'

'There's the bear with the funny nose,' Sandy interjected as he battled with his boiled egg.

'I've done something about his nose,' Emma laughed.

'Eat up your egg and then you can tell me how much improved you think he is!'

Sandy led the way through the garden to a makeshift shed where Emma evidently worked away from the house. It was full of an artist's paraphernalia, brushes and old jars and squeezed-out tubes of paint jostling each other for pride of place on the work bench, while wonderfully life-like little animals looked down at them from the shelves along the walls. Sandy went straight to a table in a corner, standing before it with a look of awe in his round blue eyes.

'Can I really have it?' he asked, gazing at the beautifully carved figure of a little bear without actually touching it.

'I made it especially for you.' Emma's voice was exquisitely tender.

When she looked at Sandy her eyes lost much of their hardness and she was no longer cynical. Her work evidently meant a great deal to her and she had carved the little bear with love in her heart. Looking at her, Katherine saw Emma's rather plain face transfigured by her affection for the child, a little boy who might have been her own.

Hastily she turned away to examine the other sculptures and suddenly there were tears in her eyes. It seemed as if Sandy had been a frequent visitor to the hotel when all was well with his parents' marriage and he had been happy and content there with Emma. And Emma herself? There was a strange new glow about her as she spoke to the child which could be a reflection of what she felt for his father.

They're not suited, Katherine thought—the arty-crafty Emma and down-to-earth Charles!

Emma came to stand by her side.

'I hear you're going to Glassary,' she said.

'I'm being *taken* to Glassary!' corrected Katherine. 'Charles thinks I'll be safer there under his command. It's outrageous, of course,' she added angrily. 'It's going right back to the Middle Ages when people did these things!'

Emma smiled.

'He won't keep you at Glassary any longer than he can help,' she declared. 'You'll be free to go as soon as your car is repaired, I understand. Charles isn't the ogre you appear to think him and he's far from being the feudal overlord, believe me. He's a very busy man, as a matter of fact, running an estate and a lucrative business in Edinburgh into the bargain. Don't underestimate him.'

She turned back to Sandy, who was now clutching the wooden bear.

'Your work is beautiful,' Katherine said impulsively, 'but why are so many of your sculptures unfinished?'

Emma looked thoughtful.

'Let's say I'm out of inspiration,' she decided. 'It sounds better than having to admit that I'm lazy.'

The bitterness had crept back into her voice, although she still looked at Sandy with a fondness which could not be denied. It would be little use appealing to Emma for understanding, Katherine thought, far less help.

Charles came in search of them.

'Time to go,' he said. 'I'd like to make Glassary before lunch.'

'I've got a bear!' Sandy rejoiced, slipping his free hand into his father's. 'An' he's got a stick to help him walk.'

'Is that what it is?' Charles laughed, glancing in Emma's direction with a twinkle in his eye.

'Perhaps he's a lame bear,' suggested Sandy with a frown. 'Perhaps he needs a stick to help him.'

Charles turned away, a look in his eyes which Katherine found difficult to fathom, while a dark, angry colour stole into Emma's cheeks.

'I hope we'll see you again before you go back south,' she said to Charles. 'I hope there'll be no more complications.'

Charles was looking idly in Katherine's direction.

'I don't think so,' he said. 'We've got the ball in our court now.'

Mrs Falkland came to say goodbye.

'I'm glad we met,' she said unexpectedly, holding Katherine's hand for the conventional few seconds. 'I expect you'll be continuing your holiday as soon as your car is repaired.'

There was an odd, waiting silence before Katherine answered.

'I haven't come very far out of my way,' she confessed, 'and I had no very definite plans.'

She knew that she would have been rejected if she had appealed to Morag for help because, like Emma, Morag would be firmly on Charles's side, but she felt that she could have asked Emma's mother for understanding. Perhaps Mrs Falkland had known Coralie quite well in the past and liked her.

Charles opened the back door of the Rover for her to get in, reserving the front passenger seat for Sandy.

'Hop in!' he said. 'I suppose you want to steer.'

Sandy raised adoring eyes to his.

'Can the bear sit beside me?' he asked.

'Where else?' Charles said his goodbyes, looking directly at Emma. 'We'll see you at Glassary soon, I hope?'

'Whenever I can get away.' She put a hand over his. 'Goodbye, Chay!'

They travelled for the best part of an hour, going deeper and deeper into the mountain fastness, with giant bens crowding the skyline and flashes of bright water shining through forest trees. Charles handed over a road atlas.

'There's no reason why you shouldn't know where you're going,' he said. 'We're travelling east, but we'll go south again in a couple of miles.'

Katherine pored over the road map, her head bent to conceal the expression in her eyes. She could not fathom this man's disposition, at one moment severe, the next warm and understanding, especially when he looked at the child. It had been the same when he had looked at Emma and, to a lesser extent, her mother. There was understanding, but there was something more. Had a long and abiding friendship turned eventually into love?

It was something she could only speculate about, not something she wanted to understand, she told herself defiantly.

Soon they were turning into a hidden glen, following a silver thread of water until they were finally at their destination. Katherine held her breath when she first saw Glassary, thinking that a more remote place could hardly be imagined. Remote and beautiful. She gazed at the surrounding peaks closing in the dark stretch of loch water and the turreted house set above it on a grey crag. The ultimate fortress, she thought with sudden alarm, a grim citadel which looked as if it might contain an ancient dungeon surrounded by an impregnable wall.

In the bright light of day, however, it smiled at their approach, and Sandy at least was happy to be there.

'Can I go to see Fudge?' he asked excitedly, forgetting Emma's gift of the bear.

Charles smiled.

'All in good time,' he agreed. 'We've been fattening him up for you!'

The blue eyes regarded him lovingly.

'Did he miss me awf'lly?' Sandy wanted to know.

'Ponies and little boys generally miss each other!'

Again the face of understanding, Katherine thought. Charles really did love the child and therein lay the ultimate tragedy. However much they pulled apart, Coralie and her former husband had this much in common; Sandy was their only child, the little boy they must have loved in the beginning with all their hearts, one accusing the other with merciless intent because they both wanted him whatever the consequences. Because they loved him they would tear themselves apart all in the cause of love.

Studying the dark face of the man behind the wheel, she tried to see more than determination in the steely eyes and protruding jaw, but what she saw still disconcerted her. Then, as the morning sunshine still dazzled her eyes, she looked beyond him to the shadows cast by the surrounding mountains on the grey, turreted house above the loch.

'Why have you left my car so far behind?' she demanded as they approached it along a narrow spur of rock which stretched like an arm into the water. 'Surely there's a suitable garage nearer this—this fortress?'

Charles smiled at the words she had chosen as he drove steadily towards his home.

'I left it at Killin because there's really no great hurry,' he said evenly. 'I mean to keep you in "this fortress", as you call it, until I can convince myself that you're no longer a danger to us, that you're not the sort of person I think you are.'

'What does that mean?' Katherine demanded when she recovered her breath.

Charles considered her through his driving mirror, meeting her challenge with a faint smile.

'It means that you and I think along the same lines,' he said. 'You evidently despise me for taking Sandy away from his mother and I feel sure that you intend to trick us whenever and however you can. I don't believe you were coming to Scotland entirely on holiday at the right moment; I think your sympathies were with Coralie all along.'

She gazed at his unresponsive back view, aware that her futile anger only amused him, and then she, too, was looking ahead at the house they were approaching.

'It's completely feudal!' she declared in exasperation as he drove the car over a stone bridge which spanned the narrow arm of the loch. 'Your attitude—this place—everything that's happened in the past twenty-four hours! If it wasn't such a nightmare I'd believe it impossible,' she rushed on. 'Are we really on an island?'

'Not quite,' he shrugged. 'There's a narrow neck of land at the north end, but I'd advise you not to use it. The bridge is the only way across.'

Katherine looked down at the shining water surrounding the house as they crossed the bridge and at the belt of pines which sheltered it from the north, aware that she would have loved this place if she had come to it under happier circumstances. The old grey stone kissed by the sun could have seemed welcoming and friendly and real contentment might have blossomed from its stillness and peace.

'It's your family home,' she said.

Charles Moreton nodded.

'I was born at Glassary,' he said. 'So was Sandy, for that matter, and my brother, whom you'll meet very soon.' A frown creased his dark brow. 'I wouldn't say he's the most hospitable of men,' he added, 'but you must work that out for yourself.'

They were almost at the house, skirting a semi-circular lawn which divided the two carriageways, and Katherine saw the grey façade of Glassary clearly for the first time. A stone canopy supported by stone pillars guarded the doorway between two long mullioned windows which looked out on either side of it, watching for strangers, no doubt, and there were four other similar windows along the front of the house and six above on the first storey, while at each corner stood a round tower crowned with a little turret of grey slate.

An elderly woman came to the door.

'This is Mrs Stevas,' said Charles. 'She'll look after you while you're here.'

Mrs Stevas didn't look at all like a gaoler, Katherine thought as Sandy rushed towards her to be enveloped in a gigantic hug.

'I've got a bear!' he announced excitedly. 'A little wooden bear!'

'There won't be any prizes for guessing who made him!' Mrs Stevas smiled, stepping back into the hallway. 'And none for guessing where your first port of call will be once you've had your lunch!'

'To see Fudge!' Sandy cried. 'Has he been lonely while I've been away, Mrs Stevas?'

'He's been eating his head off—with grief, if you like!'

The housekeeper turned to Katherine. 'If you'll come this way, miss, I'll be showing you to your room,' she added conventionally. 'You must want to get settled in after so long a journey,' she said. 'I'll feed the bairn while you're having a wash.'

Whatever explanation Charles had offered her about their unexpected visitor, Mrs Stevas appeared to be the soul of discretion, too good a servant to show her feelings at a first encounter.

Katherine looked round for Charles.

'He'll be off to the Stable House,' Mrs Stevas said. 'Mr Fergus will be waiting.'

'Is—Mr Fergus his brother?' Katherine asked.

'His *younger* brother.' The housekeeper underlined the relationship as if it was very important. 'You'll be meeting him as soon as you've had a meal. He doesn't come to the house at lunchtime because he can't walk that distance more than once a day. He has the electric wheelchair, of course, but he's stubborn about using it. Like all men, he thinks it diminishes his dignity in some way or other. We're always telling him it won't be for ever, but I don't think he believes us. Even Dr Farquharson has a job with him at times, though he's much better than he was in the beginning. You'll like Mr Fergus,' she concluded with a smile. 'Everybody does.'

They climbed a wide flight of stairs adorned by a red carpet which shone like a ruby against the dark mahogany of the panelled walls, and Katherine wanted to ask Mrs Stevas a thousand questions, although she knew that not all of them would be answered. Instead, she concentrated on the layout of the house which could become her prison for a number of days.

The stairs went up to a wide landing where they branched right and left to the upper storey of the house along a corridor with doors on either side.

'Glassary is a very old house,' Mrs Stevas explained, 'but this is the sunnier side. The family always slept here when they were at home, but now it's mainly for guests.'

Katherine wanted to laugh out loud at the misnomer, since she was far from considering herself a guest.

'We're a long way from the main road,' she suggested instead. 'Glassary is really isolated. My car broke down,' she hurried on to explain, although she had a strong suspicion that Mrs Stevas knew all about her odd adventure. 'It was too late to have it towed to a garage last night, but I'm hoping something can be done with it quickly. You see,' she added carefully, 'I'm on holiday and I had hoped to get to the Trossachs this morning.'

'You're not so far away from them.' The housekeeper opened a stout mahogany door near the end of the corridor, 'You'll be quite comfortable here in the meantime.' Some of Charles's determination had tinged her voice. 'There's no need for you to feel isolated,' she added cheerfully. 'There's plenty to do at Glassary if you have a mind to look for it.'

The words might have been some kind of warning, yet Katherine felt that Mrs Stevas could easily be won over.

'If there's anything more you might need just ring the bell,' she said, turning to go. 'Jamie will bring up your suitcase in a wee while and lunch is at one o'clock. It's a meal everybody pleases theirselves about—generally cold venison or salmon because the men are out—but they manage to make up for it at dinner time! Mr Fergus is in by then, too.'

Wondering about 'everybody', but not prepared to ask, Katherine inspected her room. Although somewhat forbidding with its heavy Victorian furniture standing round the walls and a large half-poster bed dominating the centre of the floor, it was completely adequate, and there was a smaller apartment leading off it which she discovered to be a bathroom. Quite a modern bathroom, she noted, with a handy shower and glazed waterproof curtains tucked into the bath.

All mod. cons! she thought whimsically, although she was half inclined to look for a barred window.

Maybe if I had a strong sense of humour I'd be able to

see the funny side of all this, she thought, as she crossed the bedroom to look out of the casement window to the hills. No need for bars, she decided, seeing the long drop to the gravelled drive beneath her.

When she had washed her face and tidied her hair she went back to the window as if drawn there inevitably. It was the only way of finding her bearings and working out her escape.

The short gravelled drive held out its arms to embrace the lawn with the wooden bridge which spanned the narrow neck of water behind it, while beyond the bridge the gravelled approach road led eventually to the road through the glen. There was nothing complex about it, but the fact of Glassary's isolation stood like a barrier between her and the outside world. Without a car there would be little hope of getting away even if she did appeal to Mrs Stevas for directions and possible understanding.

She was still at the window when Charles Moreton made his appearance on the approach road. He was driving a Range Rover with two dogs in it, both black and white collies who sprang to the ground even before he had drawn up at the front door. She heard him reprimanding them as she stood back from the window. He had come from the Stable House, she supposed, where he had no doubt put his brother in the picture. Whatever Fergus Moreton turned out to be like he would be this man's strongest ally.

Within minutes there was a brisk knock at her door.

'Come in!' she commanded, but was completely unprepared for Charles acting the part of porter. 'I—Mrs Stevas said Jamie would bring up my case.'

He deposited it in the centre of the room.

'I wanted to talk to you,' he said.

'Yes?'

He prowled round the half-poster.

'When you've had something to eat I want you to meet my brother.' He stood gazing across the room, his dark face devoid of expression, but somehow Katherine knew that what he was about to say affected him deeply. 'A year ago he had a serious accident and he isn't completely recovered. He avoids strangers as much as possible, so I hope I can trust you not to make your sympathy too obvious. Above all, he abhors pity. What he did was beyond the bounds of affection,' he added, 'but I've no intention of burdening you with the details. He's prepared to meet you because you've been brought here on Sandy's account, but that's all. Can I ask you to understand?'

'I'll do my best.' She looked back at him without anger this time. 'I'm sorry about your brother. Does he manage to work on the estate?'

'He's an artist,' said Charles. 'A considerable one, I'm led to believe by the people who know about that sort of thing, and he can sell most of his canvases as soon as they're finished. He and Emma Falkland are very much alike: they would prefer to keep the fruits of their labour but they realise how uneconomic that is. They produce them at local exhibitions and sell through the hotel. It's quite a lucrative idea when they get round to it.'

'I can appreciate the point of them not always wanting to sell their work,' said Katherine, thinking back to her meeting with Emma. 'A great many artists would rather give their work away, like Emma did with Sandy's bear.'

'Ah,' he said, 'but Sandy is special where Emma is concerned! He's having his lunch, by the way, and then he'll have a nap while we have ours. Afterwards, I'll take you to the Stable House.'

'It's part of the estate, I suppose?' Katherine suggested.

He nodded.

'Within riding distance. We keep Sandy's pony down there.'

'Fudge,' Katherine remembered, thinking that Sandy must have lived happily at Glassary in the past, learning to ride on a stout little Highland pony which had become his greatest treasure.

She followed Charles down the staircase, deciding to leave her suitcase unpacked. I mean to run, she thought, as soon as ever I can.

They passed a curtained alcove in the hall.

'The phone is in there if you want to use it,' said Charles.

'But I thought——'

'That you were being kept a prisoner?' His steely gaze came down on hers. 'In no way,' he said, 'but I need your co-operation. I think I've made that clear. Till your car is fit for the road again you will remain at Glassary, but you're quite free to use the telephone, even though it's only to contact Coralie in your own time to report.'

A slow colour dyed her cheeks.

'I'm not prepared to lie about that,' she countered steadily. 'I do mean to get in touch with Sandy's mother, if only to tell her where he is.'

'She won't come back here,' Charles said grimly. 'She knows the score only too well.'

His uncompromising manner where Sandy's mother was concerned disconcerted her even when she knew him prejudiced.

He must have phoned ahead from the hotel, because a substantial meal was set out in the mahogany-panelled dining-room which could have seated twenty or more with ease.

When they had made their choice from the cold dishes set out on the sideboard, Charles sat down at the head of the table and Katherine pictured a family gathering in the long room, each member with his tale to tell on his homecoming, a happy family, close-knit, and looking towards the mother of the house for love and support. She would have sat in the high-backed chair at the foot of the table, a gracious presence, eager to share their individual joy, but that chair was now conspicuously empty. Coralie had vacated it without compunction.

Charles Moreton's father would have sat where Charles was sitting now, with the portrait of a man behind him who was surely his father and Charles's grandfather. The family likeness was unmistakable, with the same dominant aquiline nose and identical penetrating gaze, the same high forehead above thickly aggressive brows, dark men in their own dark environment of brooding loch and mountain and glen gazing down the long table at the children who had crowned their marriage with love and contentment and the woman who had made it all come true. However far their ancestry went back in this one spot they would all have looked the same, their mutual air of supreme confidence stemming from their superiority in the past, from the ancient clan system which bred such men in the days when courage meant something more than lip service to a cause and when blood was thicker than water wherever a name was shared. Dark deeds had been done in these hidden glens, like the treacherous Massacre of Glencoe when the Campbell hordes had swept down on their neighbours who had offered them hospitality on a winter's night, slaying them, one by one, in the darkness, or the killing of James of the Glens, who must have trodden these mountains in his youth as Charles Moreton had done. In those days there had been many sons to carry on the family name, but now there were only two—Charles and his brother Fergus.

'When you're ready,' said Charles, looking down the table to where she sat. 'I can hear Sandy chafing at the bit out there on the terrace, waiting for us.'

The child's clear, resonant voice reached them through an open window, wondering how long they would be, and Mrs Stevas answering him.

'You must have patience, Sandy. You'll have all the time in the world to ride Fudge from now on.'

Katherine got hastily to her feet.

'He's so eager to go,' she said.

Charles had said that the pony was kept at the Stable House and the house itself was a reasonable ride away. How far? she wondered, shrugging into her coat which had been left in the hall.

They went along the edge of the loch by a well-defined path which wandered through a shrubbery of rhododendrons and azaleas in full bloom, a breathtaking glow of vivid colour which she had glimpsed from the window of her bedroom when she had first looked out.

'It's beautiful,' she said as they walked along. 'Just beautiful!'

'I think so,' he admitted. 'It was planned by my grandmother when she came to Glassary as a bride and she made it her life's work. Every shrub and tree had its individual place so that she could see them all reflected in the loch on a clear day.'

'Like today!' said Katherine, drawing in a deep breath of the pine-laden air. 'It's—almost perfect.'

'But you qualify the perfection,' he said, looking down at her as Sandy skipped ahead of them.

'I was thinking of freedom,' she answered. 'Sandy seems to have it now.'

'It's his by right.' Charles's tone was grim. 'No one but Coralie would wish to deny him all this.'

He looked about him with pride, and Katherine could only agree with him, thinking that if she had come to Glassary in different circumstances she would have loved it as he did.

The Stable House stood at the edge of the loch reflected in the mirror-like surface of a tiny bay. It was long and low, with an open stone staircase at one end, giving access to a sizeable loft whose windows looked back to Glassary through the trees. The corresponding windows on the lower floor were all open, suggesting that someone worked there for most of the day in ideal conditions if he happened to be an artist.

Fergus Moreton came to the open door of the house in a wheelchair. The impact of his handicap was something she had not expected, but she had been forewarned by his brother not to show pity. Dressed in shabby jeans and a rough brown shirt, Fergus was small and bearded, with dark, sombre eyes and dark hair growing thickly on a well-shaped head. Younger than Charles by several years, he looked the elder of the two, the brown eyes haunted by a memory.

Sandy ran towards him, arms outstretched.

'Daddy!' he cried, 'I've come back!'

It seemed minutes before the words penetrated Katherine's mind. Fergus, and not Charles, was Sandy's father! The possibility had never occurred to her, because Charles's own attitude to Coralie had been so harsh and it had been Charles, after all, who had come to London in search of her.

Looking at Fergus now she knew why. Quite apart from his physical disability, he wouldn't have it in his nature to persecute anyone, she thought.

In the first few minutes of their meeting his whole attention was centred on his son, caressing him with his eyes while his hand fumbled with the fair curls which must have reminded him of Coralie, but presently he looked up at his other visitors, at the brother who owed him so much and the girl who had returned his child to him, unwittingly though it may have been.

'Will you come in?' he asked, looking straight at Katherine. 'You've had a long walk.'

Charles led the way into the house which had been converted from an old stable block, and Katherine thought how homely Fergus had made it look. Flagged with stone hewn from the surrounding hills, the entrance hall was long and narrow with the main rooms opening out of it at the far end. The one they entered was square and low-raftered and dominated by a huge stone fireplace where logs glowed warmly between ancient iron dogs and an ample skin rug covered the floor. Deep, comfortable-looking armchairs covered in cream linen flanked the fireplace and were repeated here and there in the room beside polished tables which mostly held books. Books that were read, Katherine thought, from cover to cover and sometimes again and again.

Fergus had propelled his chair down the hall in their wake, and now he produced a tray with drinks on it: orange juice for Sandy and a home-made concoction for his brother and their guest.

'It's elderberry wine,' he explained to Katherine. 'We make it every autumn, enough to last a year. If you don't like it I'll get you some tea, though there's nothing much to eat except biscuits.'

'We had an excellent lunch,' Katherine assured him, accepting the glass he offered, 'but this looks delicious.'

Obviously Fergus had abandoned the Stable House as a home to live in, returning each evening to Glassary, where he had been born, but he had been determined to retain a presence there with his work. Through an open door she could see a studio and the untidy clutter of a cultured man who had come to terms with the life he was now forced to live, glad of the work he was still able to do and the friends he had kept.

'You stayed with the Falklands last night,' he said to Charles. 'How are they? Did they send any message?'

'Morag did more than that,' his brother assured him. 'She sent you a jar of honey, and Emma promised to pay us a visit as soon as she could.'

'She's the busy one,' Fergus mused. 'Always with something to do, though I think she should widen her horizons a bit. We've spoken about a shared exhibition in Edinburgh one of these days, but I can't pin her down to a definite date so far. She's a clever artist, but she just seems to be content where she is.'

'Maybe that's all she wants,' Charles suggested. 'She has a full life with her sculpture and the hotel.'

'Maybe,' Fergus said thoughtfully, 'but sometimes I think she would be wise to look for more. She has a tremendous talent, you know, something that should be shared with a wider and maybe more appreciative public.'

'You should talk!' said Charles, standing beside his chair. 'Hiding your own light under a bushel as you do!'

Fergus smiled at Katherine.

'My brother is prejudiced,' he said.

'Perhaps you would let me see your paintings,' she suggested tentatively. 'I'm quite sure they're good.'

Fergus hesitated, a look in his candid brown eyes which she found difficult to meet.

'They're average,' he said. 'But come and see.'

Sandy took his hand.

'Can I ride Fudge?' he asked. 'He must be tired waiting for me.'

Charles ruffled his hair.

'I'll saddle him up for you,' he offered.

Katherine was left alone with his brother, not in the least disconcerted by his handicap. Fergus propelled the invalid chair as easily as he would have walked beside her, leading the way into the studio to show her where he worked for most of the day. It held all the essentials of his art, paints and brushes and easels propped against the walls, some with completed pictures on them waiting to be varnished, others supporting boards ready for use. One huge canvas caught her eye. It was a picture of the loch on a winter's day in subtle shades of grey and blue with snow capping the surrounding hills and one ray of pale sunshine escaping between the clouds. Somehow it seemed symbolic of this man's life, and she felt quick tears stinging at the back of her eyes as she looked at him. Fergus had come up behind her and was assessing his masterpiece over her shoulder.

'It's Glassary in one of its less generous moods,' he explained.

'When everything seemed dark,' she said.

'Sandy was the one ray of sunlight.' He moved across the room. 'Perhaps I was too possessive, but how are we to know?'

'You must have loved Coralie very much——'

'Yes,' he said when she hesitated. 'I was shattered when she had to go, but now I know that it was more or less inevitable. She had her own life to lead and she couldn't hope for the fulfilment she wanted here at Glassary. I was confined to my wheelchair,' he added. 'It was—constricting for us both.'

'But Coralie——' Katherine pulled up short of saying

what she thought this time.

'Coralie was talented in so many ways,' he said. 'She had a duty to follow her particular star.'

But no right, Katherine thought, aware that she was seeing Coralie in an entirely new light.

'We've all got to have the courage to make our own decisions, though I couldn't see it at the time,' said Fergus.

'And Charles can't accept it even now!'

'Don't blame him too much.' Fergus turned to the far side of the studio where the north light flooded through the windows. 'He had reasons of his own.'

'He's dedicated to this place,' Katherine said.

'Can you blame him? If I had been the heir to Glassary I would have felt the same.'

'Why has he never married?'

Fergus drew a deep breath.

'For a good many reasons,' he said. 'But I think he will, in time.'

Without actually snubbing her, he had brought their conversation to a close. He would not discuss his brother's reason for remaining a bachelor, even if he did know it.

'I've often wished I could paint,' Katherine said. 'There's so much to be said besides the obvious things.'

'Is that what you discovered looking at "A Shaft of Sunlight"?' He nodded towards the canvas on the far wall. 'Emma sees beneath the surface, too, but she hadn't much to say about "Shaft". You met her, of course?'

Katherine nodded.

'Under difficult circumstances, I'm afraid,' she suggested. 'You know why I'm here?'

'Because Charles felt you were helping Coralie.'

Her gaze was locked on his.

'What about you?' she asked. 'You're Sandy's father.'

He nodded.

'I don't hold you responsible for what happened,' he said slowly. 'Coralie and I are to blame. I needed Sandy, though, but Coralie may have needed him more than we did. We had the legal right to keep him at Glassary.'

She looked at him askance.

'You mean you had full custody?' she asked incredulously.

'Oh, yes. There was never any question about that. It was part of the legal settlement.'

'And the reason why Charles was so determined to have him back, why he came to London in search of him.'

'What else could we do?' Fergus gripped the arms of his chair, his eyes remote. 'I couldn't go myself. You see that, of course.'

Katherine nodded.

'Coralie—I thought that Charles was trying to kidnap him,' she amended.

'Why would he do that?' Fergus asked. 'Coralie had reasonable access to him, but she refused to part with him after the allotted time. It was my ex-wife who was doing the kidnapping, but I find that an ugly word to use. If I thought Sandy would fare better in her keeping I would let him go, but alas, I don't. I believe he'll lead a better life here at Glassary, where he belongs.'

It was also what Charles believed. The fact that Coralie had lied to her as well as tricking her into helping her shocked and angered her, but it was really what Charles thought that mattered. He still believed her capable of aiding and abetting his sister-in-law, and he was not so generous as Fergus seemed to be. He would never believe that she had been tricked, because she had seemed more than willing to help, and she had accused him mercilessly while she still believed him to be Sandy's father. He would not be able to forget that, however she tried to explain it away.

'I wish there was some easy solution,' she said to the man beside her. 'Some logical way out.'

'I've wished the same thing many times,' he confessed, 'both before and after my accident. We all hope for a painless solution, don't we? It's part of our escape mechanism. "Dear Lord, don't let it happen to me!" I think

I'm over the worst of Coralie now, but I can't be sure. Did you know her very well?'

'I don't think I really knew her at all,' Katherine decided.

He seemed perplexed by her admission.

'Yet you helped to get Sandy away from London. Perhaps you felt that you owed Coralie some kind of debt?'

'I made a promise,' she said, 'on the strength of an old infatuation—a schoolgirl crush, if you like—and I'm still not sure what I should have done.'

'You feel that you should keep your promises once they're given?'

'Something like that,' she confessed. 'I feel that Coralie ought to know where Sandy is.'

'Have you been in touch with her since you left London?' he asked.

'No,' said Katherine. 'I phoned her flat several times and didn't get a reply.'

'Was she living alone?' He seemed impelled to ask the question.

'No. There were two other girls—photographic models, I think. One of them owned the flat and charged the others rent, but they were often away on assignments abroad, I gathered.'

'Do you think that Coralie may have moved out?' he asked. 'She was a restless person and there could be another man.'

The thought hurt; she could see that, realising that he had not quite got over his first love. It was still Coralie as far as he was concerned, although he knew that their marriage was over.

'I don't think there is,' she answered truthfully, 'but she did say something about having to go to New York in the near future.' Suddenly she remembered that Coralie had gone to the party expecting to meet someone important to her. 'I wish I could help,' she added lamely.

Their eyes met.

'I think you really mean that,' said Fergus. 'Anyway, you've brought Sandy back, and that's the main thing. Charles had heard the rumour about New York and we were very worried.'

He wheeled his chair to the open main door as Charles appeared from behind the shrubbery leading a small piebald pony on which Sandy sat with confidence, sheer joy shining on his chubby little face.

'Look at me!' he cried when he saw them. 'I can do it all by myself. Galloping, too!' Charles had let go of the leading rein and he dug his impatient little heels into the cream-and-brown flank. 'Here I go! Watch me!'

They watched as the pony cantered across the greensward between the house and the lochside, far too wise to gallop at speed with such a precious burden on his back.

'We'll make a horseman out of him yet,' said Charles.

'He's where he wants to be,' Fergus decided.

Katherine saw the grim look on Charles's face as she turned towards him. He agreed with his brother, but he was also determined that they would never be tricked again.

Sandy rode the pony to the loch edge and back.

'Leave him with me for a while,' Fergus suggested. 'He needs practice, and I can follow him in the chair.'

It was a concession to his son's need because he tried to use the electric wheelchair as little as possible, preferring to hobble about with the aid of a stick when he wasn't going very far. Charles gave the chair a cursory inspection before they moved away.

'He hates it, but it's the only real mobility he has at present. He perseveres with the stick, but he can't manage without the chair for very long.'

Katherine stood looking after Sandy and his father with a lump in her throat as pony and wheelchair disappeared between the trees.

'I wonder why you didn't tell me,' she said.

'Tell you what?' Charles had obviously been thinking of something more important.

'That you weren't Sandy's father.'

His face darkened.

'We didn't get that far, did we?' Charles looked back towards the loch where Sandy and his brother could be seen again on the path beyond the trees, close together now on the wider approach to a small wooden jetty where a rowing-boat lay among the reeds. 'Fergus is like that because of me,' he added grimly. 'He saved my life two years ago, ruining his own. If Coralie had been the right sort of person she would have stood by him, she would still be here—but I expect you've heard her side of the story. She couldn't live with half a man,' he added bitterly, 'so she opted for divorce—and freedom.'

'And you can never forget what Fergus did for you,' Katherine guessed. 'You're trying to make amends.'

He shook his head.

'Nothing could ever compensate for what he's been through,' he said sternly, 'so do you wonder that I haven't time for women like Coralie?'

'Did you give her a chance?'

He paused, arrested by her question, surprised, perhaps, that she should have asked it.

'More than one,' he said.

'And you'll never forgive her.' It was a statement more than a question, but he answered her.

'No. What she did was unforgivable.'

It was the sort of uncompromising reply she had expected him to make, and she knew herself cast in the same mould as Coralie in his estimation.

'I thought I knew Coralie very well,' she said slowly as they walked on, 'but people change. It's almost seven years since we were at school together.'

He looked unimpressed.

'But you were willing to help her,' he pointed out.

'And I still don't know whether I was right or wrong!' Katherine exclaimed. 'You tell me what you want me to know—nothing more.'

'I'm not given to instant confidences,' he said, 'and I

still don't trust you. I have to make sure about Sandy this time. Glassary is his home and he must stay here.'

'And you're the wealthy uncle who's invested in his future,' said Katherine. 'Coralie told me about you, but she said Fergus wanted Sandy because of the money.'

He turned towards her, his grey eyes as cold as steel.

'And you believed that?' he asked. 'You can still believe it after seeing them down there at the Stable House?'

'I hardly know what to believe!' Katherine cried, meeting his hostile eyes. 'Fergus I liked—who wouldn't?—but everything else is a confusion at present. I'm part of that confusion,' she went on unhappily, 'but I didn't mean to be. I thought I was helping Coralie. Only that, but you're never going to believe it, so why keep me here?'

Charles hesitated, seeing her distress as she stood silhouetted against the flame of an azalea in full bloom, her hair blown by the wind against the pallor of her face.

'I see your usefulness where Sandy is concerned, at least till he settles down again,' he said coldly. 'It must be something of a shock to a child to be shuttled from one parent to another at an age when he needs a stable atmosphere in a home he knows.'

'You're not suggesting that I should remain here indefinitely?' Suddenly she was thinking of Fergus whose need might be as great as Sandy's. 'I couldn't do it,' she declared.

He moved towards the house without looking at her.

'There isn't much of an alternative at present,' he pointed out. 'Your car isn't roadworthy. Where else could you go?'

'I could ask Mrs Falkland to take me at the hotel.'

'After tomorrow,' he said, 'Morag will be booked solid. It's a popular place with anglers and their wives during the spring and summer.'

'I'll ask, all the same,' she returned determinedly. 'Then perhaps I can be my own mistress again.'

CHAPTER FOUR

WHEN she phoned the hotel Morag Falkland was full of apologies.

'We haven't a corner to spare after tomorrow,' she said. 'I really am sorry.'

No doubt she was protecting Charles, playing the friend when he had asked her.

'I just thought I'd try,' Katherine said without attempting to mask the disappointment in her voice. 'Is there anywhere else I could go?'

'I think you should stay where you are,' said Morag. 'It won't be for long. As soon as your car is repaired Charles will let you go.'

Her spirit dampened by the conversation, Katherine decided to phone London again, standing in the alcove in the hall with a swiftly-beating heart which leapt in response when the receiver was lifted at the other end.

'Could I speak to Mrs Moreton?' she asked because the answering voice was unfamiliar.

'Who?'

'Mrs Moreton—Coralie,' she supplied.

'Oh, Coralie! I'd forgotten about the married bit. She's not here. She went to New York two—no, three days ago on an assignment. Can I take a message?'

Katherine's heart felt like lead.

'When do you expect her back?' she asked.

'It will all depend,' the girl on the far end of the line declared. 'If the job's any good she'll probably stay for a while.'

'But not permanently?'

'Oh, nothing's permanent, is it? Especially these days, but Coralie might be on a good thing. She's terribly ambitious, you know, and this was something big.'

'Was it designing?'

'You could say that. She was to work with a film company and if she fitted in all would be well. If not, she'll come back, I expect. Anyway, she's kept on her room here in the meantime, just in case it doesn't turn out to be as rosy as it seems. Can I say who called if she phones from New York?'

The shock she had received made Katherine feel uncertain.

'I don't think it matters very much while she's still in America,' she said. 'You could tell her that her sister wasn't at Beck Cottage when we got there and Sandy's now at Glassary.'

'Where?'

'Glassary—his father's home in Scotland.'

'Good grief!' The girl seemed taken aback. 'That's what Coralie *didn't* want to happen.'

'I know,' Katherine said quietly, 'but will you tell her, please? I made a promise and I feel responsible.'

Before she finally rang off she was aware of someone standing in the hall behind her listening to her side of the conversation.

'You were phoning London,' said Charles when she hung up the receiver.

'Yes.'

He waited deliberately, expecting an explanation.

'Coralie has gone to New York on an assignment of some sort.'

His face darkened.

'Is she coming back?'

'I don't know. I don't think anyone's quite sure what she will do.' Katherine drew a swift breath, looking him straight in the eye. 'If this job is a success I think she'll stay.'

'I see.' He didn't look particularly relieved. 'Did you also phone the hotel?' he asked.

'Yes, but you were quite right about the fishermen and their wives,' she admitted. 'Mrs Falkland couldn't take me. She pointed out that I'd be better to stay here since it would only be for a day or two.'

He made no remark, although she stood waiting.

'I saw Emma coming along the road in her Mini,' he said instead. 'She'll be going to the Stable House. Sandy's still down there with Fergus, I expect.'

'I was going to look for him,' Katherine confessed, brushing their confrontation over the telephone call aside. 'Do you want me to suggest that Emma comes back here?'

'You could do that,' he said with some enthusiasm. 'Mrs Stevas will give her tea.'

'Will you be in?' she found herself asking.

'I don't think so. I'm flying over to Mull to take a look at some property.'

She had noticed the light aircraft parked in a small clearing beyond the trees, a blue and white toy of a plane which she supposed he used in an emergency or when he was pressured for time.

'You'll be home for dinner, I suppose?'

He looked at his watch while she wondered about her use of the word 'home'.

'I'll do my best,' he said, turning away.

She walked quickly through the shrubbery towards the Stable House, hearing Sandy's delighted laughter even before she reached it. He was unsaddling the pony with the help of Fergus, who had got out of his wheelchair to lean heavily on a walking-stick, and Emma was watching them. The little tableau halted Katherine in her tracks because it seemed the most natural thing she could have come across, a man and a woman who was deeply attached to him watching the efforts of a little boy to be self-sufficient with his pony.

It was right for Glassary and the Stable House, and there could be no doubt that it would be right for Emma, but what about Fergus? Did he want to renew his attempt at marriage here, in this place, with Emma Falkland by his side?

He turned and saw her standing at the end of the shrubbery.

'Come and help!' he called. 'We need a dozen hands!'

Emma looked round as Katherine covered the last few yards to the Stable House, her face still diffused by a happy glow, although she probably wished they had been left alone for a while longer.

'I didn't know whether to call at the Lodge first or come on here,' she said. 'My mother sent you some honey. She thought she'd been rather abrupt when you phoned.'

'I understood when she said she couldn't put me up.' Katherine accepted the peace-offering with a smile. 'Charles had told me you'd be busy from now on, but I wondered if there was just a chance of a single room.'

'Not even one,' said Emma, 'but I hope we're not going to be too busy to have an hour off now and then. Had any luck with your car?'

Katherine shook her head.

'I don't think they really know what's wrong with it. It isn't new, of course.'

'You should have bought a Mini!' Emma laughed. 'They go on for ever. This one is ten years old and it never puts a foot wrong.'

'There isn't much mileage on the clock,' Fergus pointed out. 'Emma keeps it in a glass case!'

'You know that isn't true,' Emma countered. 'It takes me to Perth and back, and sometimes Glasgow. I'll buy a new one when it refuses to do either.'

Sandy ran to fetch bread and biscuit crumbs for the ducks which had gathered expectantly at the water's edge.

'What are they?' Katherine asked.

'Teal and mallard mostly,' Emma told her, 'with an occasional merganser among them. They've been breeding at Glassary for a very long time. Sandy loves them.'

Sandy came back with a tin of crumbs and broken up bread which he proceeded to throw into the water.

'Don't overdo it or they'll sink!' Fergus advised with a

bright twinkle in his eyes.

They stood watching the ducks diving for the sinking bread, their agitated rumps uppermost as they sought for it among the reeds, and then Emma took a sketching block from the Mini and began to draw. Fergus sat down in the electric wheelchair he had been using earlier to follow Sandy on the pony and Katherine found a tuft of dry grass with a stone under it where she could sit and watch.

Under Emma's inspired hand the ducks came quickly to life, but because her drawing was primarily for Sandy they were comical ducks, their actions captured by her talented pen so lifelike and so lovable that even Fergus grinned.

'You're really a cartoonist!' he declared. 'You're completely wasted at the hotel.'

'Spare my blushes,' said Emma. 'I want to get this duck just right.'

'That duck's a drake,' Fergus pointed out.

'Well, you know what I mean! If I were using colour you wouldn't have to guess,' Emma reminded him.

'Funny how the male animal world is generally the more colourful,' Fergus mused. 'It's only the human male who's so drab.'

'Perhaps he feels safer that way.' Emma stole a glance at him. 'Safer from predators.'

'Woman as the pursuer, you mean?' Fergus flung back his head to laugh, showing a row of splendid teeth. 'Has it come to that?'

'I wouldn't know,' said Emma, averting her gaze. 'There's a lot of Women's Lib about.'

'Not in these parts,' he declared, teasing her. 'We still like to believe in the dominant male—in spite of wearing the kilt!'

'You've put me off my duck!' Emma laid aside her sketching block. 'Are we being offered tea?' she enquired.

'Certainly.' Fergus picked up the discarded drawing, looking at it thoughtfully before he folded it and put it in his anorak pocket. 'Will you do the honours, as usual?' he asked Emma.

'I ought to go back to Glassary,' said Katherine.

'Why?' he asked. 'It's early yet.'

She had wanted to give him some time alone with Emma, but he had refused it. Katherine did not know what to think as she followed them to the Stable House.

Emma knew her way about, finding a teapot and some tea which he kept for just such an emergency. She also found orange juice for Sandy and some cake.

'Mrs Stevas baked it yesterday,' Fergus explained. 'She thinks I neglect myself down here.'

'What have you been doing since I last saw you?' Emma enquired, appearing from the kitchen with the tray.

'This and that,' he said. 'Nothing really special.'

'Which means you've been wasting your time!'

'I've been thinking,' Fergus confessed. 'About the future,' he added.

Emma set the tray down beside his chair.

'Does that mean you really will send your pictures to Edinburgh?' she asked, delighted.

'Some of them.'

'Why not all?'

'My dear Emma, I have dozens of them in there, some of them not yet finished.' He looked towards the studio.

'Finish them, then, before the exhibition,' she urged, pouring Sandy's orange juice. 'You're hardly being fair to yourself,' she added on a more serious note.

'I'm lazy,' he excused himself. 'Always have been.'

'You've had other things to think about,' Emma allowed, 'but now you haven't a leg to stand on if you refuse to go ahead with your work.'

'I wish I had your faith in my painting,' he said.

'Don't pretend you haven't any faith,' she returned almost angrily. 'You *know* you're good. We all do, only you need prodding occasionally,' she concluded clumsily, her colour heightening.

'I must remember that,' said Fergus, smiling at her gently. 'You were always good for me, Emma, where my work was concerned.'

The quiet words seemed to put her away from him and Emma knew it. She turned to the window to look out across the loch where the mountains came down close to the shore.

'It would be such a waste,' she said, as if to herself.

When they had collected the used cups and saucers on to the tray Katherine went to the kitchen with her to help to wash up.

'It's a shambles!' Emma groaned, looking around at the disarray of unstacked plates and pans left carelessly on the cooker hob. 'A man's idea of paradise, I suppose!'

'We could tidy up,' Katherine suggested.

'It would be like this again tomorrow, so there's not much point,' said Emma, stacking cups. 'Fergus loves it.'

'Did he always live at the Stable House?' Katherine asked without thinking.

'After he married Coralie. Before that he was at Glassary. Mrs Moreton was alive then,' Emma explained, 'and Charles was working in Edinburgh. When Charles came back Fergus and Coralie moved to the Stable House, but Coralie never liked it. She couldn't accept the fact that Charles was the real heir and Fergus was only second in command.'

'What happened to Fergus?' Katherine asked.

Emma turned her head away.

'There was an accident with Charles's plane, the one he had before the Cessna. They were flying home together from London. It was a filthy night and Fergus was at the controls. He couldn't see a thing and they both knew he could hit the mountain coming in to land. It must have been a terrible decision to make, but they hadn't enough fuel left to go back to Glasgow. It was Charles who took the final decision to land at Glassary.'

The sharp, staccato sentences fell into a silence pregnant with horror as Emma stared into the past.

'It happened quite quickly,' she went on. 'A wind had got up, but it didn't quite blow the mist away. Then, suddenly, something went wrong and they came plummetting down to destruction. It was all over in seconds. Fergus was thrown clear, but he crawled back to get Charles out. The plane was an inferno, but he managed to drag him clear before he collapsed.'

'They must both feel glad to be alive,' Katherine whispered.

'I think Charles still wonders why he should have come out of it unscathed,' Emma said, 'but he did. Fergus hauled him out just before everything blew up, but he was severely burned and his spine was damaged. At first they thought he'd never walk again,' she added. 'It seemed that he'd lost everything he believed in—his career, his art—and Coralie.'

'It must have been terrible for everybody concerned,' Katherine murmured with profound pity. 'And for you, Emma.'

Emma turned from the sink.

'I could have cheerfully killed Coralie when she left him,' she admitted. 'It was so callous—so cruel—but all she thought about was herself and her precious career, the chance she had to shine in her own small way.'

'There was Sandy,' Katherine said. 'She must have wanted to be here with him, too.'

'That was her problem. She couldn't make up her mind about motherhood. She wanted a child if he wouldn't interfere with her career. She was the most selfish person I've ever known, but I suppose I'm hopelessly prejudiced. Always have been,' Emma concluded sharply.

'I suppose Charles feels that he owes Fergus an eternal debt of gratitude,' Katherine suggested, seeing the whole sad story in a new perspective.

Emma nodded.

'That's why he made sure of Sandy's future by settling what he could on him,' she said. 'He saw it as a very small return for what Fergus had done for him. He tries all the time to do something more, but there really isn't much he can do. I don't think he'll marry now,' she added, looking straight at Katherine.

A hard lump rose into Katherine's throat.

'Is that his token sacrifice?' she asked huskily.

'It could be. Even if he did fall in love he would consider Fergus's needs before his own. He's made that way.'

They went back to the studio where Fergus was stacking canvases into two neat piles.

'You really mean to submit them!' Emma exclaimed, her eyes glowing with satisfaction.

'I'm doing as you say,' he smiled. 'And that ought to please you, Emma!'

'It does! Really, it does,' she said. 'It's a beginning.'

When they had finished their tea she drove off in the decrepit Mini, happy to have proved her point, while Katherine stayed to help Fergus with the canvases.

It was amazing how quickly time flew past and how easily they worked together. Fergus apparently did not bear her a grudge, watching her with Sandy with a smile on his lips.

'Emma will make a horseman out of him in the end,' he mused as they sat in the sunshine to draw breath. 'She's very good with children.'

'She's certainly good with Sandy,' Katherine agreed, 'but who wouldn't be? He's a darling!'

Fergus gave her a long, searching look.

'I'm glad you brought him back,' he said.

A hot colour forced its way into Katherine's cheeks.

'You know I didn't do it willingly,' she pointed out. 'I ran as soon as I knew I was being followed and it was only by the sheerest coincidence that Charles eventually found me.'

'He knew you intended to holiday in the Trossachs,' Fergus reminded her, 'and there aren't so many roads in this part of the world. When he lost touch with you in the Lake District he was very angry, but I think he feels better about everything now you're here. Mission accomplished, and all that!'

Above their heads the sound of a light aircraft coming

in to land broke the silence of the hills and they saw the Cessna returning like a white homing bird against the blue of the sky.

'I suppose we ought to get back to Glassary,' said Fergus, although he did not stand up immediately, and Katherine called to Sandy who was playing beside the jetty.

'If your car is going to be out of order for some time,' Fergus said thoughtfully, 'why don't you stay here for the rest of your holiday?'

'I couldn't!' Katherine's decision was spontaneous as she turned to face him. 'It would be quite impossible because I came here as a prisoner in the first place. Once Charles feels that I can't do any more harm he'll want me to go.'

Fergus considered the position with his head on one side.

'It's all or nothing with Charles,' he commented, 'but when you really get to know him you'll recognise how kind he can be. I'm a great burden to him, as you can see,' he went on, 'but every day I'm getting more and more independent.' He looked back to the open door of the studio. 'Now that Emma has forced me into it I must try to sell my paintings to a wider public and make a new life for myself.' He leaned over to touch her hand, his dark eyes asking the question even before he put it into words. 'Stay and take care of Sandy for a while, Kate. You'll be doing me a favour.'

She drew back as if she had been stung.

'I wasn't doing you any favour when I took Sandy away,' she reminded him, 'and you don't really know me, Fergus. Charles doesn't trust me—and perhaps neither should you.'

He smiled into her stormy eyes.

'We've made a mistake,' he said. 'I can see that.'

'Charles can't.' Her voice was curiously shaken. 'He'll never be able to forgive me for London.'

His fingers closed over hers.

'Stay, all the same,' he said earnestly as Charles came towards them through the shrubbery.

When Katherine turned he was striding across the rough grass which served the Stable House as a lawn and his eyes were as stormy as her own.

'I've been suggesting to Kate that she might stay out the remainder of her holiday with us even if she does get her car back in the next few days,' Fergus said, looking from one of them to the other. 'We're near enough to the Trossachs here; she could go off for days.'

For a moment it looked as if Charles was about to refuse and then his thoughts seemed to switch to something else as he glanced at the electric wheelchair which had been his brother's sole means of propulsion for so long.

'Just as you like,' he said without looking in Katherine's direction. 'It will be company for you.'

Fergus didn't seem to be surprised by the remark, but Katherine wondered if it was the logical reaction of Charles coming upon them as his brother had taken her hand. The confusion that rushed over her at the suggestion had nothing to do with Coralie or her part in taking Sandy away from London. It had to do with Charles and that indifferent, almost mocking kiss he had pressed against her lips as they had said goodnight on her doorstep.

The memory scorched her as she stood there, her heart in a tumult of indecision as she met Fergus Moreton's eyes. He was so unlike Charles, so quietly forgiving, that she could not help but like him, yet it was only Charles who could send her pulses racing with a look and make her furious with a taunting word.

After two days, because she felt vaguely unhappy about his attitude, she was almost glad when he had to leave Glassary for Edinburgh.

'Will you go by road?' she asked, wondering if she dared suggest that he might take her as far as Killin to enquire about her car.

'I'll be using the Cessna. It's quicker by air,' he said

after a moment's hesitation.

'I was thinking about my car,' she told him.

'If they had got the spare part from Glasgow they would have telephoned,' he said.

She watched him go down to the field where a short grass runway accommodated the plane and saw him circle over the Stable House in a brief salute to Sandy and his father, who would be watching for him. There was no matching salute for Glassary, however. She meant nothing to him at all, except a present encumbrance which he would be glad to shed as quickly as possible.

Anger and humiliation stirred in her at the thought. Fool that she was, why was she remembering so much that could only be an irritation to him? He was sufficient unto himself here in this mountain stronghold where he had sought to keep her prisoner while he made up his mind about her, and now he seemed willing to let her go, although Fergus had intervened with his suggestion that she might stay.

Fergus and Sandy returned to the house to collect Charles's car.

'We're going down to the hotel,' said Fergus, 'to select some of Emma's sculpture for my exhibition. Would you like to come?'

'I don't think so.' Katherine's voice was not quite steady. 'Emma won't be expecting me, and I thought I'd like to explore the glen if nobody objected to me borrowing the old bike in the garage for a couple of hours.'

She had made her decision on the spur of the moment, not only because she believed Emma would be happier if she didn't go to the hotel but because she wanted to get as far away from a deserted Glassary as she could. Out on the moor above the glen she could be alone to think, to make what plans she could for the future.

'Are you sure you won't come?' Fergus asked, getting out of the chair to hobble towards the garage with the aid of his stick. 'We'll be staying for tea, I expect, and I'm sure Morag would like to have you.'

'You'll be busy and I might only be in the way.' She walked beside them. 'Do you mind about the bike?'

'Of course not! Help yourself,' Fergus invited. 'It belonged to my mother and Coralie used it occasionally when she couldn't have the use of a car.'

He could speak of his former wife without pain now, and Katherine felt glad.

'You'll have to pump up the tyres,' he warned. 'It hasn't been used for over a year, but I think the brakes are all right.'

When they had gone, waving vigorously as the car went across the bridge, Katherine wheeled the old bicycle round to the house where Mrs Stevas greeted her with some dismay.

'You're not taking that old thing!' she exclaimed. 'You'll be risking your neck. It hasn't been on the road for months and it wasn't new even then. Originally, it belonged to old Mrs Moreton who used it to get about the glen when she stopped riding, and sometimes Mrs Fergus went out on it, but not very often.'

'I'll be quite safe,' Katherine assured her. 'Maybe I could go as far as Killin to ask about my car.'

'I wouldn't attempt it,' the housekeeper said, aghast at the very suggestion. 'You'd be cycling into traffic once you reached the main road.'

'I'll be all right,' Katherine repeated. 'I won't go out of the glen, if it will make you feel better.'

She had wanted to escape, she realised as she cycled away; she had wanted to put as much distance between herself and Charles Moreton as she could because he had so many reasons for distrusting her.

It was a considerable distance through the glen, cycling uphill most of the way, but the track was good, beaten as it was over rock with giant boulders standing out here and there to break up the bogland in between. Although she found herself slightly out of breath on an incline, she pressed on in anticipation of the remembered joy of free-wheeling on a downwards stretch with the wind blowing through her hair. It was the kind of freedom which brought back her childhood, although her heart had been lighter then.

If she was running away from Charles she told herself that she had time to get over it before he returned to Glassary. She had a whole day, perhaps even more.

Side tracks went off to lonely crofts, more of them than she had expected as she wondered about the people who lived in the glen. Contented people, she thought, hard-working and sincere, who took joys and sorrows when they came with the same quiet acceptance.

It was a day of fast-gathering cloud without much sunshine, but she revelled in the freshness of the air and the sense of unlimited space which the hills afforded. Perhaps over the next incline she would come across another road into a wider valley where the track would lead her away from the moor.

The final hill was a long one and she met it with her head down, pedalling hard until she came to the summit, only to realise that she was suddenly in cloud, but although she knew that she ought to turn back she allowed herself to think of the heady exhilaration of freewheeling downhill, even without a wind in her face. For up here there was no wind; only the pall of cloud that was like a thin white scarf lying gently against the hillsides.

It wrapped itself closely around her as she cycled on, but now she could feel the track going downhill as she went off into the valley of her imagining, the wide green valley of a brighter hope.

Once or twice she heard a dog bark and the bleating of unseen sheep, but they must have been at some considerable distance, because she could not see them.

Rapidly the bicycle gained speed, the momentum carrying her downwards at an alarming pace until she came to a sharp bend at the foot of the hill. She had applied her brakes half way down, but they had little effect and she shot head-first into the bank.

She lay in the heather for a long time, stunned by the

impact of her fall and scarcely daring to move in case she would find that she had broken an ankle or injured a knee in this deserted spot where there was no sound and no other movement but her own. She lay with her eyes closed, conscious of the pain in her hand and an aching right shoulder, and when she finally opened them she could see no further than the road. Her vision was distorted, for it seemed that the hills on either side of the valley had dissolved into a nebulous grey mist which had crept towards her across the moor.

When she realised that it was indeed a mist she struggled to her feet, brushing the fronds of heather from her skirt and the hair from her eyes. Still she could see nothing but the thin, swirling mist, like a veil drawn over the hills and the track down which she had come winding to nowhere. The length of time she had lain in the heather was no longer a burning issue in her mind; she knew that she would be trapped if she didn't find her way back to the glen as quickly as she could.

The bicycle lay in the ditch, its front wheel buckled, and nothing she could do would right it. For several minutes she continued to struggle with it, but it was an old machine and stoutly made and she had to confess herself defeated in the end.

She began to walk back up the hill which she had flown down so carelessly, realising that she had come a long way since she had left Glassary in the early afternoon. Trying to calculate the miles she had covered was very little help because she had covered them with ease, but now she had only her own two feet to rely on and no clear visibility to show her the way.

Gradually the mist descended, shrouding the moor in a pale grey cloak, and soon she would not even be able to see the path ahead. Instinctively she stopped, listening for some sound that would guide her, like the barking of a dog, but the awful silence of the moor seemed to stretch away into infinity, leaving her standing there like a blind person who could not even feel her way to safety.

Desperately she climbed another hill, feeling the dampness of the mist against her skin like fingers touching her. It was thicker now, more obscuring, so that she could scarcely see the track, but she could feel its metalled surface under her feet and took courage from the fact.

Trying to remember the last croft she had noticed on the hillside, she stumbled on, thinking that it couldn't be far away, but there was no obvious track on either side for the next half hour and by then she felt exhausted. The mist was everywhere: in her eyes and her lungs and clinging to her hair and her clothes. Little beads of it dewed her brow and she shook them off, only to find them forming again immediately.

When she saw the path her heart gave a great bound of relief. Somewhere up there on the hillside was the croft she had seen as she had cycled carelessly by!

Walking quickly and blindly, she stumbled over stones, almost groping her way until the barrier of a hedge loomed up in front of her, greyer and more impenetrable than the mist, but spelling safety. She found a rickety wooden gate lying half open and the walls of a house took shape behind it.

Almost sobbing with relief, she pushed her way through to find that the door of the little house was also ajar, with no light to be seen beyond it. She had come to an empty croft, long since abandoned by its former owner and standing derelict and forlorn in the swirling mist.

She stood looking at its sagging roof and uncurtained windows, and somehow the deserted building made her feel more alone than she had felt on the road, but it was her only refuge. She knew how dangerous it was to wander on under such conditions, to miss the track, perhaps, and stumble into a waiting bog.

Pushing the door wide, she paused for a moment to listen, but there was no sound and she felt her way into a narrow hall, then through another creaking door into a small room at the back which boasted a dark monster of a stove and an abandoned table which she leaned against to get used to the comparative darkness. The mist seemed to have penetrated even here and she saw that the window-pane was broken, letting in the damp, thick air.

For another hour she crouched beside the stove with no way of lighting it even if she had been able to find wood or twigs to make a fire. She was more cold than she had ever been in all her life before and her eyes began to droop heavily.

Whether she slept or not, propped against the stove, she was never quite sure, but suddenly she was arrested by an unusual sound. It came in drifts, above her and around, fading away just when she realised that it must be the engine of a plane coming in over the hills. Charles returning in the Cessna to find her gone!

She sprang to her feet, wanting to go to meet him, but how foolish that was! He would be nearing Glassary by now, turning the little plane into the landing strip and walking up to the house where Mrs Stevas would be waiting for him.

The minutes fled away. It was quite dark now, with the mist, like a blanket, pressing against the window. Katherine went to the front of the house, staring out, trying to penetrate the grey wall in front of her, listening in the quiet for the slightest sound.

When it came it sounded like the distant beat of hooves, and suddenly she knew that it was just that. Someone was going down the road on a horse.

She ran then, stumbling in the darkness, aware that the sound was going gradually away from her, but when she pulled up she heard it again. Whoever—whatever—had passed was coming back. She was still standing on the narrow track leading to the croft when horse and rider loomed in front of her.

'Katherine!' Charles exclaimed, getting down from the mare's back.

'Charles! Oh, Charles——!'

She was in his arms, pressing her head against his wet shoulder, holding on to him for all she was worth.

'I found the bicycle,' he said roughly, not putting her away. 'Why did you leave the road?'

'I thought—if I got to the croft I'd find shelter there, but it was empty.' She could hardly form the words for sheer relief. 'I knew it was dangerous to wander about in a mist.'

'We'll have to go back there,' he said. 'For a while, anyway, to give the mare a rest. She came up the glen like the wind, although sometimes we couldn't see a yard ahead of us. I can't ask her to go back all that way with the mist thickening. We'll be safe enough at the croft for a while.'

He led the way back up the track with the mare's bridle over his arm and a steadying hand under Katherine's elbow.

'I'm sorry,' she said, aware that he was deliberately making light of their predicament. 'I should never have taken the bicycle. I should never have left Glassary.'

He didn't answer that, pushing open the door to let her go into the croft ahead of him, and she went gladly this time, feeling herself safe. It was some minutes before Charles followed her in.

'I've tethered the mare in an outhouse of sorts,' he explained, 'and I've found some wood. We'll have a fire going in next to no time, though I can't promise you anything to eat. I left Glassary too quickly to think about food.'

'It doesn't matter.' She stood watching as he held his lighter to the damp wood he had collected. 'Surely we won't be here for ever.'

'No.' His tone was abrupt, although he would not blame her for the predicament they were in. 'Mists have been known to lift in an hour—or settle in for days. There's no wind.'

'I'm sorry,' she repeated, believing him impatient. 'I had no idea this would happen or I wouldn't have attempted to come so far.'

She could still feel the comfort of his arms about her in

that first moment of dissolving fear when his face had been close against her wet hair and she had known herself no longer alone, but now they stood apart again, gazing down at a reluctant fire.

When it burned up a little she could see his face more plainly, but it was without expression.

'Come nearer,' he said, making room at the fire. 'We may have some time to wait.'

Sitting with his back against the table and his arm round her for added warmth, he supported her as her eyes closed. She was utterly exhausted by the trauma of the past few hours and ready to accept the comfort of his arms.

When she woke her head was against his shoulder, his long legs thrust out towards the fire which was already dying in the grate.

'You've been asleep,' he said, moving his cramped position, 'and the mist's lifting.'

Katherine heard the sound of the wind, then, sweeping down the glen, and the rush of it through the broken panes of the window, and she listened to it with regret and a vague, hopeless longing in her heart.

'Time to go,' said Charles, damping down the remains of the fire. 'We should be able to see the road quite clearly now.'

The rising wind had banished the mist, driving it down the glen before them and a furtive moon lit their way. They reached Glassary before midnight, to be greeted by Fergus and Mrs Stevas in the doorway, both deeply concerned for their welfare.

'Thank goodness you're back!' Fergus exclaimed. 'We were beginning to get nervous.'

'You'll have had nothing to eat,' Mrs Stevas said practically, 'but I've a meal ready in the kitchen.'

Charles helped Katherine down from the mare's back.

'What happened?' Fergus asked. 'Are you hurt?'

He was looking at Katherine, his dark eyes searching her face, and Charles turned abruptly away.

'We were trapped by the mist for a while,' he said brusquely. 'Katherine had sheltered in MacNiven's old croft and we had to stay there till it lifted a bit.'

'You'll be hungry,' said Fergus, putting a hand on Katherine's arm. 'If I know Mrs Stevas there'll be plenty to eat in the kitchen.'

'It's all ready,' the housekeeper assured them. 'Hot soup and an omelette when you're ready.'

Fergus was still looking keenly at Katherine.

'Are you sure you're all right?' he asked anxiously. 'You look ghastly. Better get off all those wet clothes and get into bed. Mrs Stevas can bring you a tray.'

'I don't want to cause any more trouble.' Katherine was gazing at Charles's unresponsive back view. 'There's been enough for one night.'

'Don't think of it as trouble,' said Fergus. 'We've been worried about you, but now everything is in focus again. When Charles came back with the Cessna we were still at the hotel and we had his car, but a horse is often the best mode of propulsion under the circumstances.'

Charles had ridden the mare hard, galloping where he could in his attempt to find her, and once again she tried to thank him.

'I don't know what I would have done if you hadn't come,' she said. 'I was almost at my wits' end.'

His mouth hardened.

'You would have survived,' he said as Fergus hovered in the background waiting to offer her sympathy and understanding.

Why was there so much difference in Charles now that they had returned to Glassary? All the tenderness, all the concern he had shown when he had first found her out there on the moor was gone and the glimpse he had allowed her of another side to his character had faded, making her wonder if it had been no more than wishful thinking on her part when he had seemed so tender. It had seemed very real at the time. She could still remember the touch of his hand as he helped her back along the path to the deserted croft and the concern in his voice as he had assured her that all was well. That was why she had been able to sleep so fearlessly with her head cradled on his shoulder.

Because it was difficult to see everything in its true perspective, she accepted Fergus's suggestion that she should go to bed, but she still hadn't adjusted her thoughts when the two men followed her up the stairs an hour later. The tray Mrs Stevas had brought her was still across her knees and she was wide awake.

The brothers paused at the head of the stairs, obviously finishing a conversation they had begun in the kitchen over their shared meal, and then, in the silence which followed the closing of a door farther along the corridor, there was a light tap at her door.

Her heart bounded at the thought of Charles, but it was Fergus who came in.

'I wondered if you were asleep,' he said, 'but you look a lot better, I must say. You'll have forgotten about everything in the morning.'

It would be difficult to forget, Katherine thought, smiling at him as he hobbled across the room.

'I missed you,' he said, his dark eyes sincerely concerned. 'I wish I'd been able to help.'

'Charles did everything he possibly could.' Her tone was unconsciously harsh. 'There was no point in everyone being upset, and I'm quite sure he was angry.'

He stood beside the bed for a moment, looking down at her as he sensed the drama of her return.

'Why bother to fight Charles?' he said. 'He won't keep you here any longer than he needs to. You see, he's got to be sure you won't spirit Sandy away on Coralie's behalf a second time. You know I have the legal right to my son, don't you? One day I may be able to adjust my thoughts and learn to live without Coralie, but at present the fact remains that I'm still in love with her in a kind of a way. She's Sandy's mother and I can't really expect anyone to take her place quite so soon. I'm completely handicapped in many ways, Kate,' he sighed.

'You're a brilliant artist,' she protested, defending him against himself. 'That ought to count for something.'

'It helps,' he admitted. 'I sell some of my pictures and it makes me feel independent up to a point, but I can never really deny the debt I owe to Charles.'

'He believes it's the other way round,' she said huskily. 'You saved his life once.'

'Oh, that!' He brushed the fact aside. 'It was one brother for another. It shouldn't involve a debt.'

'I can imagine Charles being determined to pay it, all the same,' said Katherine.

'You know he's settled a good deal of money on my son?'

'Yes. I knew that in the beginning.'

Fergus paused.

'Charles considers Sandy his heir, but that's a great mistake,' he said. 'He could marry and have children of his own. Coralie was a bad example, I'm afraid, and he's the determined type.'

The fact that Charles was merely using her to further his own ends struck coldly against Katherine's heart. He imagined that Fergus was attracted to her, but how could he be on so short an acquaintance? Three days was no time at all to reverse a man's conception of love, and Fergus had already told her that he hadn't quite got Coralie out of his system.

'Goodnight, Fergus,' she said quietly, holding out her hand to him.

He crushed her fingers in his.

'Thank you for looking after Sandy,' he said gratefully.

CHAPTER FIVE

It was two days before she spoke to Charles again. The cattle mart at Dalmally had taken up a good deal of his time, but he also seemed to be avoiding her when he was at Glassary. They met at meals, but Sandy and Fergus and Mrs Stevas were there, too, so they had no opportunity of discussing anything of a personal nature until they came face to face on the second evening.

The day had been warm and sunny, a perfect spring day with the promise of more to come, and Katherine had lingered outside on the terrace as long as she could. Charles drove up as she was about to go in.

'Have you had a good day at the mart?' she asked.

'Excellent. Prices were good and everyone was in a jovial mood. Farmers are either broke or happy with their success. I sold all the sheep we took down and bought several ewes with followers. Lambs,' he amended when she looked slightly puzzled.

'I've a lot to learn.' She smiled as he got out of the Range Rover to stand beside her. 'I like the word "followers", because that's just what lambs do!'

He looked up the glen to where the sun was shining on the hills.

'What did you expect to achieve by running away?' he asked abruptly. 'Quite apart from your car being out of action for another week till the parts come from Glasgow, I need you here at Glassary. In a new role,' he added reflectively. 'I think you could help Fergus to recover completely.'

She gazed at him for a moment as if she hadn't quite heard what he had said, her heart beating fast against her side, her thoughts in turmoil.

'What are you trying to say?' she asked at last. 'Your

brother has no wish to start another love affair.'

'I was thinking of a new start,' he said.

'Meaning?'

'He needs to regain his confidence. He needs to acknowledge the fact that there are other people in the world apart from Coralie.'

Her pulses racing, Katherine turned to face him.

'Are you suggesting that I might pick up the pieces of his broken life?' she demanded. 'Are you really asking me to—to compensate Fergus for all he's suffered through Coralie? Do you expect me to do it because I helped Coralie and deceived you in the first place?'

'I'm making a suggestion, nothing more,' Charles answered, moving towards the house.

'I don't think Fergus needs me.' She walked beside him, determined to have her say. 'He'll make his own decision in the end. He's your brother,' she pointed out with a wry smile as they reached the foot of the stairs.

Sandy came sliding down the broad banister-rail and he caught him in his arms.

'That's enough of that!' he reprimanded. 'Particularly when you're alone.'

Sandy looked at Katherine.

'Is it dangerous?' he asked, hoping for her support.

'I think you ought to do as you're told,' she said. 'If your Uncle Charles says it isn't safe, I think he knows best.'

The wide blue eyes studied her for a moment while her advice sank in.

'I've had my supper,' Sandy said, dismissing the incident of his joyous descent from the floor above to the back of his fertile little mind. 'It was chicken soup an' cabbage.'

'What? No meat?' Charles laughed. 'That's no way to treat a hungry man!'

'Did you buy some new lambs?' Sandy wanted to know since he was now properly forgiven.

Charles nodded.

'Several. They came with the ewes.'

'I'll see them in the morning,' said Sandy, climbing the stairs again as Fergus made his appearance at the dining-room door.

'Had a good day?' he asked, looking at his brother. 'Did you sell what you took to Dalmally?'

'The lot,' said Charles, turning to mount the stairs after his nephew. 'If you'll excuse me, I'll get a wash and change while you amuse each other.'

He seemed bent on throwing them together, although Katherine had done her best to explain that she wasn't attracted to Fergus in the way he hoped she might be. Perhaps she hadn't been firm enough, but she hadn't wanted to argue with Charles again.

'Emma is pressing on with the exhibition,' Fergus told her as they walked through to the drawing-room. 'She's quite determined to include my pictures, so I expect I ought to go along with it.' He paused to look at her speculatively. 'If you're not going back to London immediately we thought you might be willing to help.'

'I'd like nothing better,' Katherine began, 'but——'

'But?' he prompted.

'I don't know the first thing about art,' she excused herself, because she seemed to be walking into a trap of Charles's making.

'That wouldn't matter one bit,' Fergus declared. 'We wouldn't expect you to discuss my pictures—perspective and sensitivity and all that rot. You'd be on the selling side and Emma or I would be there for reference if a critic did get you into a corner. You really don't need to go back to London, I gather, so won't you consider it?'

'I wish I could.' She sat down on the settee where he had settled himself. 'But you know how Charles feels about me. He can't trust me, and all this is—sort of family, isn't it?'

'That's rubbish!' he exclaimed. 'We've known you for almost a week now and it stands out a mile that you're perfectly honest.'

Tears of gratitude for his trust welled in her eyes.

'It's kind of you,' she said, 'but this is Charles's home. I can't stay for ever.'

'You can't leave, either, until your car is repaired,' he pointed out, 'so you've at least got a day or two to make up your mind about the exhibition. Emma can't be in Edinburgh for more than a week because of the hotel and I'd like to be with Sandy as much as possible, so you see how essential your help would be. We'd fix you up in Edinburgh in Charles's flat.'

'No! I'd rather not do that.' She sat looking down at her clasped hands. 'I'd rather be completely independent,' she added.

'Which sounds as if you might consider my idea?' he suggested happily. 'It would help a lot, believe me, and you needn't worry about Charles. He seems to be leaning over backwards to please me at the moment, which probably has something to do with that debt of gratitude you spoke about.'

He was not entirely blind, Katherine thought. He had seen the trend of his brother's reasoning and was half amused by it.

'Can I think about the exhibition?' she asked. 'There must be plenty of other people you could get to help out.'

'Not as many as you might think for so short a time,' said Fergus. 'If it was a local showing it would be easy enough, but people aren't prepared to go so far afield as Edinburgh for just a couple of weeks. It would mean staying over there, for one thing, and farmers' wives are far too busy in the spring to leave home, however arty-crafty they may be during the winter months.'

'It was just a thought,' Katherine said, already warming to the idea. 'How long would it be for?'

'Three weeks in all. We'd need the extra week for packing everything and bringing most of it back! We won't get the gallery for longer than that,' he explained. 'They're in big demand, especially in the summer and leading up to the Festival. You'll love Edinburgh,' he added, as if she had already accepted his offer. 'It's a magic city at any time of the year, but it comes into its own in the spring—like Paris.'

This new enthusiasm in him was what Charles had been waiting for and Katherine realised that she could not ignore it. For the first time since the accident Fergus was turning his face to the sun, giving himself a second chance, and his brother would do everything in his power to further it.

'You make it sound tempting,' she heard herself saying. 'What does Emma think?'

He looked at her, perplexed by the question.

'Emma? Oh, she'd be all for it,' he declared. 'She knows she couldn't be in Edinburgh all the time herself because Morag needs her at the hotel and she'll be as grateful as I am if you take it on. Well—nearly!' he laughed when Katherine looked doubtful. 'Emma doesn't enthuse very much and neither do I, but this means quite a lot to her, I guess. Neither of us have ever been part of a professional exhibition before and this will be breaking new ground for us both. Maybe it won't be such a howling success this first time,' he added, 'but at least we've tried.'

Katherine got up to look out of the window.

'That's it, isn't it?' she said. 'Trying. I know it's all going to work out for you,' she added almost passionately. 'It has to!'

'It will,' he said, getting up to stand beside her, 'with your help.'

It looked as if she had made her final decision as far as Edinburgh was concerned, and Charles would probably be pleased with the effort she had made. For one thing, it would mean the end of her sojourn at Glassary, and that was something he must surely want.

Thinking about the events which had led up to their meeting and the conflict which had existed between them ever since, she decided to phone London again in another effort to contact Coralie, who had been the instigator of it all. The number rang out, but there was no immediate response, and she was about to put the receiver down when someone spoke from the far end. It was a man's voice, high-pitched and effeminate, and for a moment Katherine wondered if she had dialled the wrong number.

'Coralie?' he said when she asked. 'Oh, my dear—yes! Coralie Edgar, of course. You know she went to New York?'

'Yes, I know,' said Katherine. 'I'm phoning to ask if she's come back.'

'Not yet, dear,' the voice said. 'She may be staying over there for some time, you know. For a week or two, anyway. She has this marvellous assignment which ought to put her on her feet for a long time. It's décor, you know, dear. Quite a feather in her cap, I would say, and it could lead to greater things. She's always wanted to get to the top and she's on her way.'

Katherine stood holding the receiver with a sense of shock.

'Does that mean she won't be coming back at all?' she asked.

'Oh, dear me, no! If she can get a chance of work in London she'll be right back, I would think. New York is a wicked place, dear—so full of disappointments and broken promises. Nobody cares, really. It's all a great big melting-pot of talent without a soul. Coralie knows that one job has to be backed up by another and she would be better nearer home for a while. Can I say who called?'

'It doesn't really matter,' said Katherine. 'I'll ring again.'

She turned from the telephone to find Charles waiting in the hall.

'I was trying to contact Coralie,' she told him.

'And?' His mouth was grim.

'She's still in New York.' She drew a deep breath. 'Charles, I don't really know what to say about all this,' she confessed, 'but if you did want to get rid of Coralie it seems that it's all worked out to your satisfaction.'

'You think she won't come back?'

'I can't be absolutely sure, but you've got Sandy now, and that's the most important thing, isn't it? He's back at Glassary where he belongs, with his father and you.' There was a sudden forlorn note in her voice. 'I don't suppose you'll ever forgive me for helping Coralie,' she added, 'but please remember that she tricked me, too. When I first met you in London I believed in her.'

'You weren't the only one to be taken in,' he said grimly. 'We all were, but I think Fergus is getting over her now. He's far more relaxed and looking to the future. One day he'll marry again, I hope.'

'Will that set you free?' she asked. 'Free from your sense of obligation,' she added when he didn't answer immediately.

'I don't know,' he said eventually. 'All I want to be sure about is that he'll come out of this without scars.'

'I think he will,' Katherine decided. 'He's not the sort of person to linger for ever in the past regretting what has happened to him. He has far more courage than that, and once his talent has been fully recognised I think he'll put it all behind him and learn to live again. He has so much to look forward to, Charles, and so many people eager to help.'

'Including you and Emma,' he suggested with a brief smile which did not reach his eyes. 'That should make a difference.'

'If I can help I'll be more than willing.' Suddenly she had made her decision. 'Fergus has asked me to go to Edinburgh for the Exhibition to arrange the commercial side of things, and Emma will help with the pictures.'

'Where will you stay?' he asked after the barest of pauses. 'I have a flat in Heriot Row eating its head off for want of an occupant. You and Emma would be welcome to stay there.'

She turned her back on him.

'It's good of you to offer, Charles,' she said, 'but I couldn't accept. You've been kind enough while I've been here, more than kind when I looked on Glassary as a prison at first, but I can't let you feel responsible for me any longer. I'll find somewhere to stay in Edinburgh without difficulty, I dare say. It'll be a sort of extension of my holiday.'

'After which you will go back to London?' he queried.

'I suppose so.' She made the decision without enthusiasm. 'I'll have to look for a permanent job.'

After that brief encounter with Charles the days fled away with lightning speed as their preparations for the exhibition took shape, occupying all their time.

'We're lucky to get it in before the Festival fever begins,' said Fergus as they wrestled with their choice of exhibits. 'Otherwise we wouldn't have a hope. Keep me from getting too excited about this,' he added boyishly. 'I'm half-way to the Academy already, so you'd better hit me on the head to bring me down to earth again!'

'Fergus,' said Katherine, 'you'll never be anything but modest, whatever happens! I'm going to put on my clairvoyant hat and tell you it's all going to be a huge success and everything is going to turn out well for you and Emma. Her little animals are beautiful. They're bound to make an impression and I think they'll be a sell-out in the end.'

'It would give her a tremendous lift,' he said more seriously. 'Emma has never been able to get out of the domestic rut for long, but she's an artist to her finger tips. You'll never hear her boast, but these little sculptures of hers are something special.'

Emma came and went between the Stable House and the hotel, quietly busy as she collected the best of his canvases to transport them to Edinburgh in good time for the exhibition. She seemed to be glad of Katherine's assistance, yet oddly wary of her, and Katherine supposed that she was a basically friendly person who had taken her on trust after a fairly short acquaintance and wasn't completely sure if she had done the right thing. Emma worked like a Trojan, more for Fergus's sake than her own, but even in the rush of preparations for such an important venture she found time for Sandy, carving him lifelike replicas of seals and an otter for his collection when she was not too busy at the hotel.

Fergus, who had been teaching his son to fish, took him out on the loch in a boat, which seemed a risky sort of adventure when he could never keep still, and Katherine watched them with a vague longing in her heart, thinking that everything would be much the same at Glassary when she had gone. The old house would still be there on its green promontory overlooking the loch; the ducks would still bob in and out among the reeds, and an eagle would soar high above the mountains, while Sandy and Fergus and Charles would remain, happy in each other's company, as they were now. It was almost impossible to look at them without pain now that she knew she was in love with Charles.

The conviction haunted her as she went about the small routine tasks she had accepted at Glassary—helping Sandy to dress each morning; setting the table for their evening meal to relieve Mrs Stevas of the extra work; going to the Stable House to carry old pictures down from the loft because Fergus couldn't cope with the outside staircase yet, and putting Sandy to bed when she had supervised his final meal of the day with all Emma's carved animals ranged in a row, looking on. Bedtime stories were also a part of this evening routine because, suddenly, they had become a family.

Watching her, Fergus seemed fascinated by the change in his child. Sandy had become almost garrulous as he recounted the adventures of his busy day, and when Charles came in he had to repeat them for his uncle's benefit, stringing out the telling of them to gain half an hour extra downstairs before Charles finally carried him up to bed.

A deep warmth had settled on Glassary and even Charles seemed to be aware of it.

'You're doing a lot for Fergus,' he told her one morning

as he saddled the pony for his nephew. 'He's even beginning to look different.'

'I can't pretend it has to do with me, Charles,' she said. 'Several things have made this difference. Being useful again is one; being independent, if you like. And then——' She hesitated. 'There's Emma,' she went on deliberately. 'They have so much in common, and this exhibition means a great deal to them. I know you're helping, too—financially—and Fergus appreciates it.'

'I'm hoping to get my money back on the deal when they've sold everything!' Charles laughed, dismissing his own effort. 'It's the moral assistance that helps most at present, the help you and Emma are giving him. Have you made up your mind about the flat?' he asked unexpectedly.

'I spoke about it to Emma, but she won't be able to stay in Edinburgh for more than a couple of days at a time because they're busy at the hotel now.'

'I was thinking about your own arrangements,' said Charles.

'Fergus knows someone who has a small private hotel in Royal Crescent.'

'Douglas Grear and his wife? You'd find it noisy,' he said, 'but perhaps you wouldn't mind that.'

Katherine turned to face him.

'Can't you see that I don't want to go on inconveniencing you?' she demanded huskily. 'I've been here on sufferance when you must have wanted Glassary to yourself, and having me in your flat would only make things more uncomfortable, especially if you wanted to occupy it yourself for the odd night.'

'It was Fergus I was thinking about,' he said abruptly. 'He'll feel better about things if he knows you're comfortable, but please yourself about the offer. I won't be in Edinburgh, I can assure you, and I wouldn't put you out even if I did want the flat. I have several friends who could give me a bed for the night, so think about it.'

Katherine finally discussed the proposition with Fergus.

'Charles has offered me the use of his flat,' she told him as they counted canvases in the downstairs sitting-room of the Stable House. 'I don't know whether to accept or not.'

'It was my suggestion,' he admitted, 'but why don't you use it? It would be most convenient for the gallery, for one thing, and you and Emma could shack up comfortably together on the odd night she could stay in Edinburgh.

'What about you?' Katherine asked. 'And Sandy?'

He looked uncomfortable.

'Kate, would you mind very much if I didn't come across very often?' he asked apologetically. 'I'm being a terrible coward about this, but I don't think I could take it if I saw all my pictures hanging there without one single "sold" notice on them.'

'That's about the last thing you need worry about,' Katherine contended. 'They'll sell like hot cakes!'

'I wish I had your confidence,' he smiled wryly. 'I think they're good, but another crushing disappointment would be more than I could take.'

'What about Emma?' Katherine asked. 'She would be equally disappointed.'

'It wouldn't be the same for Emma,' he reasoned. 'She's useful in another sphere. Morag couldn't do without her at the hotel, but I'm dispensable.'

The sudden defeatist mood surprised her a little, although she could understand it.

'I wasn't thinking about Emma's own work,' she explained. 'She would be far more disappointed if your pictures didn't sell than she would be if her sculptures remained on the gallery shelves.'

He paused for a moment to consider her argument.

'You're perfectly right, Kate,' he said. 'Emma's the greatest person I know. A true friend.'

'So it's goodbye to the fit of the blues?' Katherine joked. 'All your pictures are going to sell!'

He put an arm round her shoulders.

'D'you know, I think you're good for me,' he said, 'and you're certainly good for Sandy. He's come right out of his shell these past few days.'

'It's thanks to Emma, too, you know,' Katherine pointed out. 'He's very fond of her.'

'She bribes him!' Fergus laughed. 'With all these animals she carves for him.'

'I don't think that's her reason at all,' Katherine protested. 'She does it for love.'

He turned his head away.

'Love for Sandy,' he said. 'What else could it be? Emma's always been a caring sort of person: caring what becomes of her friends, possibly caring about me and certainly about Sandy for the past couple of years. She couldn't understand Coralie and tried to stop her when she went away. I couldn't.' He sighed heavily. 'What had I to offer her, anyway?'

'Glassary and a lifetime of contentment at the Stable House,' Katherine answered promptly.

'That would be enough for you or Emma,' he mused, 'but not for Coralie. I ought to have been able to understand her desire for freedom to do her own thing, but I didn't. Sometimes, in my wilder moments, I feel that I should have been more demanding, but it wouldn't have worked. Coralie was determined to go. She couldn't bear defeat, and I understand that more easily now. I'd like you to be at the flat with Emma,' he added, 'while I'm here with Sandy.'

It was something she had to do for him, Katherine realised, something small but important; more important than her pride.

She approached Charles about her change of mind the following morning when she found him at the breakfast table encouraging his small nephew to eat up his porridge.

'Will I be big and strong like you if I do?' Sandy was asking as she opened the door.

'Bigger and stronger, I expect!' Charles pushed back his chair. 'It could also make you pretty, like Katherine!'

Sandy considered the point.

'I don't want to be pretty,' he said. 'Just strong. I don't want to be a girl.'

Charles laughed.

'You're fine as you are,' he said, 'and we've decided to keep you.' He looked across the table at Katherine. 'When do you go to Edinburgh?' he asked.

'I wanted to speak to you about that.' She sat down opposite him. 'Can I change my mind about borrowing your flat?'

'Certainly. I thought you would,' he added, 'when you had talked it over with Fergus.'

'I'd take great care of it.'

'I'm sure you will, although you'll find it's pretty basic. A man's domain, in fact,' he warned.

'That won't matter,' she assured him. 'Emma and I will be out all day and sometimes in the evenings, I expect, and we won't be giving parties.'

'You can please yourself about the parties,' he said, 'but I would guess that you'd be far too tired for midnight flings after you've been at the gallery all day. I'll give you the key.'

While he was unfastening it from his key-ring she tried to thank him.

'It's very kind of you, Charles, especially after I'd refused.'

'It's easy enough to change one's mind. People do it all the time, and Fergus will feel better about it if you're at the flat.' The emphasis was on his brother's continuing peace of mind. 'There's a caretaker on the top floor, by the way, who controls the speaking system when the flats are empty. Do you know how it works?'

'I think so. A friend had one in London and there was one at Millie Downhill's, if you remember?' A deep colour rose into her cheeks as she mentioned the noisy cocktail party where they had first met. Where he had first learned to distrust her, she thought. 'I suppose they're all much the same.'

'More or less.' Charles handed over two keys, a Yale and a larger one for a mortice lock. 'You'll need them both,' he explained, 'when you first go in if you don't want to disturb the caretaker. The flat's on the first floor and there isn't a lift.'

Their fingers touched as Katherine took the keys and she drew back as if she had been scorched.

'You're quite sure you won't want to come to Edinburgh?' she asked to hide her emotion.

Charles shook his head.

'Not to the flat,' he said. 'I might take a look in at the exhibition once it gets going.'

'We're banking on it so much,' she confessed, echoing some of Emma's enthusiasm. 'It means such a lot to Fergus and we just can't allow him to be disappointed.'

'Not a second time,' said Charles, turning towards the door. 'I've made up my mind about that.'

Katherine could not see his face, but she could imagine the determination reflected in the grey eyes and the grim look of the mouth. They were all trying to help in their different ways and Charles was ruthless in his pursuit of repayment, seeing her as a willing tool where his brother was concerned.

'Fergus will learn to live again,' she said unsteadily. 'His life is only beginning in many ways, and he'll soon forget Coralie.'

'With your help,' he said abruptly as he went out in search of his brother.

Katherine sat quite still when he had gone, thinking that she had no right to call him back to dispute that final statement or tell him that she loved him. When she looked about her everything she saw spoke to her of Charles: the quiet, homely room where the sun came flooding in over the tree tops in the early morning; the crackling of the wood fire burning cosily in the grate; the ticking of the grandfather clock in the hall, heard clearly because he had left the door open, and probably more than everything else, Sandy, the nephew he loved. Outside she could hear the little noises she had come to recognise as essential to Glassary—the clucking of pheasant chicks in the breeding pens beyond the back door; the bleating of lambs up on the hill and the ewe's answering call and, finally, the click of the gate as Charles went through the shrubbery on his way to the Stable House to discuss the morning's work with his brother. It was his way of involving Fergus in the running of the estate, a kindness which the younger man appreciated, although she knew that Fergus looked on Glassary as Charles's kingdom and would rather stand firmly on his own two feet at the Stable House. If he could sell his pictures in a wider market that would be possible, but if not he would still be dependent on Charles till he found some other job.

They took the first canvases over to Edinburgh the following day, packing them carefully in the back of the Rover with sheets of cardboard in between while Emma followed in her Mini with her carvings in boxes and two of her larger sculptures on the passenger seat by her side. Mrs Stevas would look after Sandy, a task which she greatly enjoyed, and Charles would go his own way in the Range Rover, covering the lonely miles of Glassary to check on sheep.

Fergus was quite capable of driving, but he tired easily.

'Would you like a change of seat?' Katherine asked him when they had gone half way. 'I'd love to get my hands on that steering-wheel!'

He smiled at her thoughtfulness, a little wryly, she thought.

'We'll stop at the next watering place,' he agreed. 'Emma will have caught up with us by then and she'll be ready for a coffee.'

Emma drew up ten minutes later in the overloaded Mini.

'I thought I'd find you here,' she said cheerfully,

coming to join them at the café table. 'Does anyone want to swop cars?'

'We've just arranged that Kate should drive the Rover for a while,' Fergus explained. 'I tend to get cramp sitting in one position for too long.'

Emma looked concerned.

'You're sure you can make the journey in one go?' she asked.

'Of course! Didn't you know I was the perfect passenger when I can stretch my legs occasionally? Don't worry about me, Em,' he said. 'I'm as anxious to get to Edinburgh as you are and we need to get there this morning.'

There was enthusiasm and a touch of excitement in his voice and Katherine could feel her own anticipation mounting in sympathy. The exhibition meant so much to him and Emma, although the end of it could mean nothing but parting as far as she was concerned. In three weeks' time it would be goodbye to Charles and Glassary for ever.

Edinburgh on a Saturday morning was a hive of activity, like any great city, but the Scottish capital had an air of regality as the sun shone down on Princes Street with the Mound and the castle rising splendidly above it. The trees in the Gardens were in splendid bloom, adding colour to the scene, and high above the Calton Hill white clouds sailed across a sky which was gloriously blue.

'It's the most beautiful city in the world,' Emma said patriotically as they drew up at the gallery together. 'It's a pity we have to work!'

The little gallery had been closed for a week, but a great deal of rubbish left by the former occupants had to be cleared away, boxes and plastic containers and large sheets of corrugated cardboard which Emma husbanded for future use.

'Not that I expect us to be taking much back with us,' she said cheerfully, 'but there are still a few things to bring across on Monday.'

'I thought we'd leave the murals behind,' said Fergus. 'They're the sort of thing that's generally commissioned.'

'Not on your life!' Emma declared. 'They're almost your best effort and they'll look splendid along that back wall.'

They were inside the gallery now, having obtained the keys from the shop next door, and she was already planning the layout for the exhibition, deciding where this or that would be placed to the best advantage when she had finally studied the light.

Smiling gently at her enthusiasm, Fergus followed her from section to section leaning heavily on his stick, while Katherine tidied up the floor.

'It isn't really dirty,' she decided, wielding a broom when most of the packing material had been stacked beside the door. 'Just untidy-looking.'

There was much to be done. When they started to carry in the canvases it was amazing to see the amount of work Fergus had got through in the past three years. Most of the larger paintings had been done before his accident, but there were small gems of landscapes which he had worked on after Coralie had left.

'He put everything he had into them,' Emma said, coming up behind her as Katherine handled one. 'It was a sort of escape mechanism as far as he was concerned and I think they're magnificent. That one is the glen beyond Glassary. He could get there in the car after a while and be alone.'

Katherine had already recognised the painting and the deserted croft on the hillside where Charles had found her when she had strayed from Glassary. Fergus had captured it all so faithfully: the green of the new heather and the grey of the boulders where the river ran down, and the sun gilding the rocks above the treeline. There was even a hint of mist descending slowly as it had done that day as she had cycled along the rough hill track, but in the picture there was a shaft of light above Glassary that was like a promise.

The painting was priced at sixty pounds and she asked impulsively:

'Do you think I could have it?'

Emma looked surprised.

'If you really want it,' she said. 'Why are you so keen?'

Unable to meet her searching gaze, Katherine looked down at the picture again.

'Because I was lost up there,' she said slowly. 'You can even see the empty croft where Charles and I were forced to shelter till the mist cleared. Fergus has a keen eye for detail.'

Emma continued to gaze at her.

'I heard about it,' she said at last. 'It was lucky that Charles found you so quickly.'

'I was terrified,' Katherine admitted. 'It was so quiet, yet there were so many inexplicable sounds.'

'The moor whispering!' Emma laughed. 'We used to listen as children, scaring each other to death! Never mind—you were rescued, and that must have been the end of fear as far as you were concerned. Another human being on the scene can make a world of difference.'

Katherine could feel the comfort of Charles's arms about her as they had found each other in the darkness and her fingers tightened possessively about the ornate little frame.

'I must have it,' she said huskily. 'I'll tell Fergus.'

'His first sale of the exhibition!' Emma stuck a little red seal on the glass above the painted croft, 'He'll take it as an omen! I wish I'd thought of it first,' she added, 'because having even one "sold" seal on your work before you open makes a difference. A certain type of person will always buy if they think things are already going well, and we want to encourage them.'

At two o'clock they went out to a nearby restaurant to find something to eat.

'We can't do much more,' said Emma, 'and I'm ravenous. We haven't eaten since the café at Callander. I really am getting excited now that things are shaping up so well,' she added. 'I can see it all happening!'

'Don't get too enthusiastic,' Fergus warned. 'Otherwise you'll be more than disappointed if things don't sell out.'

Emma had arranged most of her own work on little tables between the different sections of his paintings, and it was quite true to say that everything was very saleable if only they could attract the necessary customers.

'Do we need flowers?' Katherine asked. 'Or would they detract from the exhibits?'

'Nature against art?' Emma mused. 'Perhaps they would. I rather like the stark look of Fergus's drawings against the sea-green of the walls. They're decoration enough.'

'You're right,' Fergus agreed. 'All we need is a great bank of azaleas from Glassary to hide all that glass at the entrance. Kate could bring them through on Monday morning.'

Bringing something of Glassary to Edinburgh to remind her of the glen, Katherine thought, but perhaps she didn't need a cascade of vivid colour spilling from a metal trough to keep the memory of Glassary in her mind.

It had been arranged that she should bring the Mini back to Edinburgh with the final exhibits on the Monday, while Fergus and Emma would join her on Tuesday morning prior to the official opening of the exhibition at two o'clock. They had dispensed with the idea of a celebrity to launch their endeavour, preferring to open quietly and let the public drift in as they felt inclined. They had advertised extensively and Fergus hoped that they would attract the right clientele without the added expense of a glamorous film star or a popular singing idol to speed them on their way.

'That sort of thing doesn't really attract the sort of people we want,' he said, smiling as he looked at the little red seal on Katherine's picture. 'It's buyers we want.' His eyes lingered on her flushed face. 'What are you going to do with it?'

'My painting? I'm going to keep it,' she told him, 'to remind me of these past two weeks. I'm going to hang it on a wall somewhere so that I can look at it all the time. I suppose I want to remember Glassary because, in spite of everything, I've been happy there.'

Emma turned abruptly towards the door.

'Time to go,' she said. 'Time to pack up and set out for home.'

It was after three o'clock before they had tidied the entrance, stacking the best of the corrugated sheets into the back of the Mini to take with them.

'We'll meet at Callander for a quick snack,' Emma said, getting in behind the wheel. 'If you beat me to it, as I think you will, you can order.'

When she drove away Fergus said:

'I ought to have taken you to see the flat. Did Charles give you a key?'

'The key and all the necessary instructions,' Katherine told him. 'Don't worry about me settling in. It won't be the first time I've taken over an empty flat.'

She wanted to go to the flat alone, to be there without anyone—not even Fergus—looking on when she first opened the door. It was foolish, she knew, something she found hard to explain, even to herself, but it was what she wanted.

At Callander the Mini was parked at the kerb before the café where they had been served excellent coffee that morning and Emma was ordering tea when they joined her.

'We'll be home before dark,' she assured them. 'There's plenty of time.'

It was a respite from driving for Fergus, who had insisted on taking the wheel of the Rover when they had left the gallery, and he looked relaxed and almost happy now, thinking of the effort which lay behind them.

'I'd like Charles to see it,' he said. 'Perhaps he'll drop in during the week if he has time to spare. Personally, I think he works too hard.'

'He said he might look in,' Katherine answered, feeling that his brother's concern for him brought Charles very near. 'He must want to see what you've been doing with yourself all these months,' she added lightly, 'and I think he'll be surprised.'

Emma was still thinking about the exhibition.

'We've got a good position,' she said. 'Anyone interested who was in Edinburgh even for a day couldn't fail to spot us.'

'With all Kate's azaleas in the entrance lobby they could hardly miss!' Fergus laughed. 'You're going to need the Rover to bring them over from Glassary.'

'I could give you rhododendrons if you came down to the hotel,' Emma mused. 'But no! Perhaps we'd better stick to one species and be more artistic!'

They covered the remaining distance to the glen, one behind the other, saying goodbye to Emma when they reached the hotel.

'You'll come in?' she asked, but Fergus shook his head.

'We're already late,' he said. 'See you Tuesday!'

Turning into the glen, they were conscious of its peace, of the quiet that came, like acceptance, at the ending of the day. Neither of them spoke until Fergus said unexpectedly:

'If you'll drop me at the Stable House I'll get the murals ready.'

Katherine drew up when they had crossed the bridge.

'I'll walk from here,' she offered, getting out from behind the wheel. 'There's time to stretch my legs before dinner. You can bring the Rover up when you come.'

Walking slowly through the shrubbery where the rhododendrons shone like pale lamps in the gathering dusk, she allowed the stillness of the gardens to encompass her. There was practically no sound apart from the rustle of leaves as some small creature of the night hurried across her path and a sleepy duck took to the water with a scarcely audible splash. Behind the shrubs and the still water Glassary stood waiting, and when she hurried towards its lighted windows there was a strange hope in her heart.

She came out of the shrubbery on to the end of the terrace, to stand there transfixed by what she saw. The light was still strong enough and there could be no mistake. Her car had been returned from the garage where it had been repaired and it was waiting for her outside the front door. Charles was letting her see as plainly as he could that she was no longer welcome at Glassary. It was his way of saying goodbye.

CHAPTER SIX

CHARLES was standing in the hall when Katherine went in.

'There's been a phone call,' he said, coming forward. 'Someone for you. Mrs Stevas took it and didn't ask who was speaking. It was a woman's voice, but the line was bad.'

He was looking directly at her and because she still felt distressed about the car her voice faltered a little.

'I've no idea who it could be,' she said after a moment's consideration. 'No one knows where I am.'

'Except Coralie,' he suggested. 'You phoned her several times.'

'Only to leave a message.' She met his distrustful gaze, aware of a new anger in him. 'You must believe me, Charles. I haven't spoken to Coralie direct since I left London, but I did think she ought to know where Sandy is. I'd be out of my mind with worry if he was my son and I discovered that my sister hadn't got him, after all.'

'I doubt if you would ever find yourself in that kind of situation,' he said, to her surprise, 'but that's beside the point. Do you think she'll come here?'

'I don't know. I've no idea what Coralie might do because I'm realising, more and more, that I never really knew her. It was a man who answered when I last phoned the flat, and he seemed to know quite a lot about her,' she added reluctantly. 'He gave me the impression that she'd pursue her career quite ruthlessly now that she found herself on the road to success.'

Charles nodded his agreement.

'There's just one thing,' she added, taking off her coat. 'However ambitious a woman may be, she must want her child more than anything else.'

'To trail round the world with her, leading an unnatural life?' His eyes were suddenly remote. 'We don't intend Sandy to develop into a mixed-up kid, as he would do if he were left entirely to Coralie's tender mercies. Fergus has legal custody and he's given Coralie reasonable access to Sandy in the past, but now we have to settle for the letter of the law. No more "kidnapping", as she likes to call it. This is Sandy's home. You can see for yourself how happy he is at the Stable House with his father, and when Fergus eventually marries again he'll be able to give him a normal home.'

'I don't think it will be very long before Fergus does remarry,' said Katherine, thinking of Emma and the bond which existed between her and Sandy. 'If this exhibition is a success—even if they sell only half of their work—it will make a tremendous difference to him. He wants to prove himself, Charles, to feel that he can stand again on his own two feet with no props to support him. I don't mean that he isn't grateful for all you've done for him,' she added swiftly, 'but it would help a lot if he could feel capable of supporting a wife and family on his own.'

Charles moved to the open door to look out.

'It's a natural enough ambition,' he allowed, 'and I can only thank you for your part in it.'

She tried to smile.

'Don't thank me too soon,' she said. 'I was just adding things up because—because I've become very fond of Sandy in the short while I've known him. I hope he can have the best of two worlds,' she added quietly. 'Knowing his mother—being with her from time to time—yet recognising Glassary as his true home. It's asking a lot of a child of his age to accept the fact that his mother lives such a nomadic life most of the time, but Glassary might make up for that. Its security is something that even a child could accept.'

She stood beside him in the open doorway looking out into the night and seeing only the means which would take her away from the glen.

'Now that my car is repaired I must go,' she said bleakly. 'You can't want to keep me here any longer, Charles. I've been nothing but an embarrassment to you.'

'Where will you go?' he asked without turning to look at her.

'To Edinburgh for the exhibition. After that, I don't know. I love Scotland,' she added simply. 'I'd like to stay here.'

He looked beyond the shadowy outline of her car to where the hills came down, closing in the glen.

'It shouldn't take Fergus too long to make up his mind,' he said brusquely. 'There's just one thing.' He turned to look at her, at last. 'I don't think you should tell him about the phone call when there's just a chance that it wasn't Coralie after all.'

'They'll ring again if it was important,' Katherine said, 'and meanwhile I'll try to think who else it might have been. I'd cut adrift from my old colleagues in a way after my boss died, but it's just possible that one of them might have traced me to Glassary. How, I don't know, unless they had some idea that I'd always had a love affair with Scotland!'

Her gaze followed his to the shadowy contours of the hills and the dim outline of the mountains above them and back again to the nearer quiet of the gardens where the rhododendrons still gleamed in the dark, realising suddenly that he might think she was pleading her own cause.

'There must be lots of things I could do in Edinburgh,' she concluded firmly, 'but meanwhile I'm not thinking farther ahead than the outcome of the exhibition.'

In the silence which followed her confession twin headlights pierced the darkness, heralding Fergus's approach from the Stable House.

'He's changed completely,' said Charles, turning to go inside. 'At one time he wouldn't even attempt to drive again.'

Fergus braked beside her parked car.

'That was quick,' he said, winding down his window. 'Or is it just that we don't want you to go?'

'I've had my reprieve,' Katherine tried to say lightly. 'Charles obviously feels that I can't do any more harm.'

Painstakingly Fergus edged himself from behind the steering-wheel to cross the gravel to her side.

'I never thought that you did,' he said gravely, putting an arm about her shoulder in a comforting way. 'Even when you first came here I guessed that you must be doing it for Sandy's sake and that you weren't really Charles's prisoner. The whole idea was absurd, you know. He couldn't possibly have kept you at Glassary against your will.'

'I suppose I knew that, really, but it was all rather disconcerting in the beginning,' Katherine admitted. 'I had no idea what you would be like or how—homely Glassary would turn out to be. I suppose I judged everything by Charles's attitude towards me, but I think I can understand his anger now, though not his contempt.'

'It's time he got over that,' said Fergus, pressing her hand. 'Don't worry too much about it, Kate, if he hasn't such a good opinion of women. He has his reasons, quite apart from Coralie, but that's too long a story to relate just now.'

She looked round at him, trying to see the expression in his eyes.

'He never married,' she said. 'Was it because of someone? Someone he loved and lost?'

Fergus hesitated, looking towards the house with its watching windows.

'More or less,' he said. 'Charles has a long memory.'

They walked the short distance to the door, still with his arm about her shoulders, and his grip seemed to tighten as they entered the hall where his brother was waiting. Charles turned towards the fire which Mrs Stevas had lit in the wide stone fireplace to dispel the damp, and Katherine thought it would have been the most welcoming sight in the world if her thoughts hadn't been in turmoil.

'How did your day go?' Charles asked his brother. 'Are you more or less ready to stun the public with your genius and Emma's little men?'

'The "little men" are mostly animals,' Fergus laughed, releasing Katherine as they reached the fireplace.

'I thought she'd bequeathed most of the animals to Sandy,' Charles said. 'Judging by his collection I shouldn't think she has many left.'

'She's been hoarding them for years,' Fergus returned. 'I'd no idea how many she'd made. I'm going down to the hotel in the morning to help her root out some more in case we do have a quick sale.'

'She could do them on commission afterwards, I suppose,' Charles suggested. 'How long will you be away tomorrow?'

'Why?' Fergus asked. 'Is there anything spoiling? Anything I could do here?'

Charles shook his head.

'Not a lot,' he said. 'I'll be going on to the hill to check up on some prowlers we've seen around at the weekends. They come up with innocent-looking caravans and not so innocent-looking vans and invariably there's a fleece lying in the heather where they've butchered a ewe. They don't always take the fleece with them and, of course, we've to think of the lambs. They're not big enough yet to be worth killing, but we have to protect them if the ewe's been taken.'

'How cruel!' Katherine exclaimed. 'When you think about Glassary it's hard to believe that anything so barbaric could happen up here. Who are these people?'

'Twentieth-century bandits, I suppose you could call them,' Charles answered. 'If they'd do the job cleanly I wouldn't mind so much, but sometimes they lame an animal or leave it with a festering wound in its side to die in agony as far away from human habitation as possible. But that's enough of gore for the moment,' he added. 'The point was that I can't take Sandy with me on an errand like this, so perhaps you would keep an eye on him for a while?'

He was looking straight at her, and Katherine knew that he must have seen her surprise at his request.

'I'll do what I can,' she said, 'since you appear to trust me.'

'Why not?' Fergus came to stand beside her again. 'Why not,' he repeated, 'when you're practically one of the family now?'

Charles turned his back, going slowly towards the stairs.

'You shouldn't have said that.' Katherine sat down on the wooden settle beside the fire. 'Because it isn't really true.'

'It's as true as doesn't matter,' Fergus declared, 'and I think Charles is quite prepared to trust you now that we've come to know you better. Otherwise, why would he ask you to look after Sandy?'

'Probably because he knows I wouldn't get very far if I did decide to take Sandy away again! No,' Katherine amended hastily, 'that wasn't quite fair. I think he was giving me the benefit of the doubt—because of you.'

Fergus took her hand.

'Accept it,' he said warmly. 'I'd like you two to be friends instead of enemies.'

'Is that what we are? Enemies?' The word choked in Katherine's throat. 'We were in the beginning, I suppose.'

'It's a long time ago,' Fergus consoled.

'Not much more than a couple of weeks.'

'A day can be as long as a lifetime in assessing a friendship,' he pointed out.

'I suppose it can.' She moved restlessly, freeing her fingers from his confining grasp. 'When should I start out on Monday?'

'You don't mind going on ahead?' he asked. 'Going alone, I mean.'

She shook her head, unable to answer him in words

because they were choking back in her throat. She would be going on ahead for a very practical reason, but she would also be leaving Glassary for good. She would be going alone in the fullest sense of the word.

In the morning Charles had gone out before any of them was awake.

'He's off on to the hill with the dogs in the Range Rover,' Mrs Stevas announced, 'and he's taken his lunch with him. He wouldn't have bothered if I hadn't insisted, but I made him take what would do him till dinner time. Some folk think they can exist on fresh air when they're busy,' she sniffed, 'but it can happen too often.' She looked across the room at Fergus. 'Will Emma Falkland be coming here for her lunch?' she demanded.

'No, I'm going over to the hotel.' Fergus helped Sandy on to a chair at the table. 'But you'll have Kate and Sandy to cater for, which is an even distribution all round.'

'You'll be well enough fed at the hotel,' Mrs Stevas remarked dryly, 'but no better than you would be here. I suppose you'll be back in time for your dinner?'

Katherine took Sandy down to the lochside where they fed the ducks and went for a short trip to the little island in the green-painted boat which was used for fishing. They didn't fish because Sandy made a habit of casting the fly too widely, and the day before had hooked it strongly into his trousers as it had swung back towards him. The expert in the shape of Charles had been there to unhook him, but Katherine didn't want to be faced by a more dangerous accident when they were alone. The trouser leg could so easily have been his own chubby flesh, and she could imagine the howl of anguish which would have gone up if he couldn't have been freed immediately.

As they rowed close to the shore he referred to Charles more than once, 'My Uncle Charles lets me fish' or 'My Uncle Charles is teaching me to row', but she was determined not to rise to the obvious bait. Finally 'Why isn't he here?' had her completely lost for an answer.

If she had told Sandy the truth she would have said that she thought Charles was trying to avoid her, that this final day in her presence was too much for him, but how could she offer such an explanation to a child?

After lunch, while he took his usual nap, she strolled as far as the bridge, looking out across the narrow neck to where the carriageway joined the main road and thinking that it was no longer a means of escape to her but the final way she would travel in the morning from Glassary.

How could she possibly have thought that she might stay here, she wondered, that she might have become part of this quiet, mountain-girt kingdom which belonged to one man when that man was only waiting for her to go?

Then, coming down the road towards the bridge, she saw the Range Rover. Charles was driving, with another man beside him, and in the back there was something with a tarpaulin over it. When they drew up she saw that it was a young deer lying on its side with its pathetically large eyes fixed on Charles's back.

'We've got a casualty,' he said briefly. 'Could you get some hot water and bring it to the stable? There's plenty of disinfectant there.'

She ran back to the house, her breath coming swiftly, her heart pounding with indignation. It was a young roe deer, a 'baby Bambi', as Sandy would have called it, and it was badly injured.

Like Sandy, Mrs Stevas was resting after her mid-morning walk to church and there was really no need to disturb her. Katherine boiled the water in her immaculate kitchen, carrying it along the side of the shrubbery to the stables where Charles and the ghillie were waiting.

The deer was stretched out on the canvas, still alive, and Charles beckoned her over.

'How squeamish do you feel?' he asked.

'I hate to see an animal in pain,' Katherine confessed, 'but I'll be all right if you give me something to do.'

'Hold her head as gently as you can.' He made room

for her on the floor beside him. 'Try to keep her still.'

It seemed to take an eternity to remove the bullet which had lodged in the deer's side without actually killing it, but when it was done the little animal lay back with its head in Katherine's lap and its dark eyes on her face as Charles and the ghillie bound up the wound.

'We'll let her go in the morning,' said Charles. 'She'll be all right once she's on her feet again. Can you bring some milk?'

From time to time, while he had been prodding for the bullet, he had looked quickly into Katherine's eyes, watching for the first signs of nausea, but she had set her teeth and continued to hold the deer, soothing it with soft, crooning words which it appeared to understand. She could not show Charles how sick she felt or how much she relied on his experience to heal this small, helpless creature which depended on them for its life.

Tears stood in her eyes as she went back for the milk he had asked for, and when she knelt beside him again to pour it gently down the deer's throat she knew him as determined as ever to steer her in his brother's direction because he imagined that Fergus had need of her and because he owed him a personal debt which he believed he could never repay in full.

These precious moments they had spent together tending the stricken deer would remain in her memory for ever, a tenderness she would guard for as long as she lived. Whatever the future might hold for her, there would be Charles and Glassary to look back on with a bitter-sweet pain.

When they had settled the deer for the night they walked back to the house together, and she remembered how she had thought of it in the first instance as a prison. Strange prison, she thought, when it held everything she would ever want within its stout grey walls!

'I'll be leaving fairly early tomorrow,' she said, 'and taking my own car, so this is really goodbye.'

'You'll be coming back to the Stable House,' he said

harshly. 'You can't refuse Fergus if he asks you to marry him.'

She turned away, not wanting him to see the futile yearning in her eyes.

'He won't ask anyone to marry him till he can stand firmly on his own two feet,' she declared huskily. 'That's what the exhibition is all about. Can't you see how alike you are?' she challenged. 'Determined and independent to a degree. Fergus must prove himself before he can settle at the Stable House with any hope of continuing happiness. He needs his independence and—and our help,' she declared. 'There's Emma, too. She understands him so well and she's very fond of Sandy.'

'Fergus knew Emma long before he met Coralie,' Charles pointed out doggedly. 'She was "the girl next door", but I don't think there was ever anything between them except an acknowledged affection, a brother-and-sister emotion, if you like.'

'Which could easily have developed into love,' Katherine suggested.

He thought about the idea for a moment.

'You overrate the emotion,' he said harshly. 'A full and lasting understanding is just as good.'

'How can you say that when you know it isn't true?' Katherine cried. 'I love you, but you could never return my affection because you could never trust me. You told me so in the beginning, remember? You thought that I must be Coralie all over again because I allowed her to impress me. Well, I'm not impressed any more, but I'm not going to stay at Glassary to become the answer to your regret. I must go. Emma will look after Fergus for you!'

Shaken by the confession of her love, she rushed from him into the waiting house, where she watched from her bedroom window as he plunged through the darkened shrubbery into the gathering night.

Before Fergus returned she knew what she must do. She would leave Glassary without seeing Charles again, if that was possible. They had said their last goodbyes.

He made it easy for her to go unchallenged. Emma came back with Fergus to join them for their late evening meal and as soon as it was over he made the injured deer his excuse for spending the next hour in the stable, coming back to the house when Emma had gone.

In the morning he released the deer, taking it up to the treeline to watch it hobble away to freedom in search of the herd.

By nine o'clock Katherine had packed her suitcase and was ready to go.

'We'll follow you as quickly as possible,' Fergus said. 'We're fully loaded with Emma's gear. You're sure of the extra pictures?' He looked into the back of her car. 'You haven't much space left.'

'Enough!' Katherine tried to smile although her heart felt as heavy as lead. 'I'll have everything in place by the time you get there. You don't look as excited as you should be!'

'It doesn't always show,' said Fergus, 'but I'm quaking inwardly. It's what the critics are going to say tomorrow that bothers me most.'

'I don't think you need to worry,' Katherine told him.

'Will you stay at the flat?' he asked.

'No.' She looked away from his searching eyes. 'I'd rather wait till Emma joins me.'

How could she tell him that she couldn't go to Charles's flat alone, that she needed Emma's moral support, if nothing else?

Saying goodbye to Sandy was one of the hardest things she had ever done. She bent to kiss him on the cheek, feeling his skin fresh and soft against her lips.

'When will you come back?' he asked anxiously.

'I wish I could,' she said because there was no need to lie to him. 'I only wish I could come back soon!'

Even as she drove away from Glassary she was watching for Charles coming off the hill, hoping that she would see him once more yet not knowing what she could say to him if she did.

Through her driving mirror she could see the old house dwindling in size behind her, screened at the bridge by a blazing barrier of azaleas and the quieter flame of rhododendrons as she put distance between her and Charles's kingdom for the last time.

When she reached the main road she drove faster than usual, keeping pace with her thoughts, although she had no real need to be in Edinburgh before the afternoon. When the Trossachs were behind her and the great bens had given place to the rolling Ochil hills she joined the motorway and was in the Scottish capital by noon. Driving fast, she had put as much distance as possible between herself and Glassary.

The day was fresh without a great deal of sun, but even without its gilding rays Edinburgh was an enchantment. Katherine drove swiftly along Princes Street, climbing towards St Giles with a new excitement stirring along her veins. The gallery was in the old town, tucked in between a narrow close and a shop selling leather goods which was already doing a brisk trade with the early tourists, who were mostly American or German. They haunted the narrow streets on their way down the Royal Mile to the Palace, standing to gaze at buildings which were steeped in ancient history or turning aside to admire the crafts displayed for their inspection by modern man.

Parking her car in a side street, Katherine opened the gallery door. They had worked hard on the Saturday afternoon to make everything ready, but she dusted vigorously when she had hung the remaining pictures in their allotted cubicles so that not even a speck of dust could mar their bloom. They looked so good hanging there in their selected places, land and seascapes glowing with the colours of the glens, and the odd portrait Fergus had attempted as a challenge when he had wanted to tackle something different for a change.

The portraits were undoubtedly good, but it was the pictures of the glens with their guardian mountains which said most to her, because she had lived among them for over two weeks of happiness and a wild despair which would stay in her memory for ever.

That night she spent in a nearby hotel, thumbing through the catalogue Emma had prepared in order to acquaint herself with prices and a brief general knowledge of what they were about to offer to the public.

'I feel sick at the pit of my stomach!' Emma announced when she arrived with Fergus the following morning. 'All this D-Day atmosphere is making a coward out of me before we even begin!'

'You'll get over it,' Katherine assured her practically. 'We have to remember that we can't expect to be crowded out on the very first day.'

'It's the critics I worry about,' Emma wailed. 'I won't be able to bear it if they say we haven't an ounce of talent between us, though that wouldn't be true of Fergus,' she added stoutly.

'Nor you!' said Katherine, watching Fergus as he made his final round of the cubicles. 'Must we really take a lot of notice of the critics?'

'They can make or break you, in a way,' Emma said, 'but sometimes the public can reverse their decision by just buying what they like and you have to sell.'

'Then why worry?' Katherine asked. 'I feel success in the air!'

'That's because you want us to succeed,' said Emma, prowling behind Fergus to replace a small sculpture she had picked up on her way in. 'We've got to come out of this alive,' she added under her breath, 'and preferably kicking. It means so much to both of us.'

At two o'clock they opened the gallery doors and waited. There was no immediate rush, and Katherine stood anxiously behind her pile of catalogues willing the public to come in. By three there were half a dozen people standing quietly in the gallery assessing what they saw. Two of them were obviously newspaper critics taking notes.

By five the trickle had expanded to a steady flow and they were answering questions and providing extra information on every side. Emma was sticking little red seals on her sculpture with amazing regularity, but only Katherine's small red sticker on the painting of the glen adorned Fergus's efforts.

Trying not to see his evident disappointment, Katherine busied herself parcelling up Emma's sculpture. The little animal models had sold so well that there were gaps on most of the display tables and many of the shelves, but these could be easily filled.

She saw Fergus speaking to a tall, bearded man in a blue duffle coat, and they were still deep in conversation when the gallery closed at seven o'clock.

Emma came through to the cramped little office where Katherine was unpacking another box of her sculptures.

'Well, that's that!' she gasped, flinging herself down in the only available chair. 'Our very first day!'

'You've done well,' Katherine pointed out. 'Counting gaps, I reckon you've sold about forty of your animals.'

'They're not important,' Emma shrugged. 'It's the pictures we have to sell. Fergus has been talking to that bearded wonder for almost two hours,' she reflected, 'but he hasn't bought a thing.'

When the bearded man finally shook hands and departed, Fergus put a sticker on one of his smaller paintings.

'One sale in five hours,' he remarked despondently. 'We'll have to do better than that.'

'You're suffering from first-day blues,' Emma suggested. 'Tomorrow we'll do better. Perhaps if we went out and had something to eat we wouldn't feel so gloomy. Where would you suggest?'

'The Gateway serve a first class meal and it's near the flat,' he said.

It had been arranged that Emma and Katherine would share the flat while Fergus went to a friend who had offered him hospitality as soon as he had heard about the exhibition.

'You'll be on your own after tomorrow until the weekend,' he said to Katherine when they were finally seated at a table in the restaurant of their choice. 'How do you feel about it?'

'I'll cope,' she promised. 'Don't worry about me.'

They ate heartily in spite of their disappointment, discussing the type of person who had come into the gallery on their opening day.

'Perhaps we should have had a celebrity to launch us, after all,' said Fergus. 'It's the popular gimmick nowadays.'

'And it doesn't sell a thing!' Emma decided.

'I don't know,' he answered. 'It brings people in and we do want the public to recognise us. We also need their support.'

Katherine sat back in her chair.

'Emma's done not too badly this afternoon,' she said. 'It could be your turn tomorrow.'

'True enough.' Fergus stretched and smiled. 'Will you drop me at the Pattersons' on your way to the flat?' he asked. 'I can find my own way to the gallery in the morning.'

'And just how will you do that?' Emma demanded. 'If you're thinking about a taxi you can forget it. I'll pick you up when I've dropped Kate at the gallery.'

He smiled at the new edge of authority in her voice.

'Yes, ma'am!' he agreed. 'Just as you say!'

Although the Pattersons asked them in for a nightcap, Emma declined the invitation because it was getting late.

'Have you been to Charles's flat before?' Katherine asked almost nervously as Emma parked her car in a side street off Heriot Row. 'Charles gave me full instructions when he handed over the keys, but it's nice to be with someone who knows their way around.'

'I don't,' Emma said. 'It's never really been lived in for any length of time since Charles bought it. He uses it occasionally, I believe, but it lay empty for several years after the accident. In fact, it was never really occupied.'

There was a brief pause while Katherine inserted the key in the mortice lock to open the heavy main door.

'I believe it's pretty basic,' Emma said. 'A bachelor's idea of adequacy.'

They climbed a wide staircase which spiralled up to the first floor where two doors faced each other across a landing.

'Here we are!' said Emma, halting before one of them.

A brass nameplate much in need of polishing bore Charles's name above a bell, and Katherine inserted the Yale key in the lock. Even if the flat was indeed 'basic', as Charles had first warned her, it would be adequate for their needs.

The door admitted them to a square hall darkened by the fact that it had no natural light, but Emma found a switch and it was soon flooded in the glare of electricity. Doors led off on either side, the first one they tried opening into a spacious living-room which boasted a bed-settee, several unrelated armchairs, a table and four dining chairs upholstered in green leather, another smaller table to accommodate the telephone and a standard lamp with a gold shade in a corner. Reading matter littered the dining-table at one end, firm proof that Charles took most of his occasional meals at the other, and there were more books on the table beside the telephone. The one unexpected touch was the soft, close-pile carpet covering the floor from wall to wall. Katherine had first noticed it in the hall and it was probably repeated throughout the flat, its rich deep purple the one luxurious touch in an otherwise ordinary home.

Emma was busy opening doors.

'There's only one bedroom,' she announced, 'but I can easily sleep on the settee. They're amazingly comfortable, as a rule, and this one looks new. Come and see the kitchen,' she commanded. 'It's quite something!'

The kitchen and bathroom had been completely redesigned to a fastidious taste, Katherine thought, as she noticed the built-in cupboards in natural pine and the split-level cooker that looked as if it had never been used. A woman's taste!

Someone—probably the caretaker at Charles's request—had brought in milk and eggs, and there was a loaf of bread in the metal bin on top of one of the work surfaces.

'We won't need these till the morning,' Emma said. 'I'll pop the milk into the fridge.' She switched it on, although it was completely empty. 'You can shop for the other things you'll need tomorrow,' she suggested. 'There's bound to be a lull at the gallery before the public rush in!'

'Fergus was disappointed,' said Katherine. 'He couldn't help showing it.'

'It's early days yet,' Emma decided, 'but I can't help wishing I hadn't done so well. It makes it seem as if his work isn't so important, and that's not true. They've simply *got* to appreciate his painting, because all this means so much to him.'

'I wonder if there'll be anything in the newspapers tomorrow,' Katherine mused. 'Some sort of official criticism.'

'We'll have to wait and see.' Emma prowled restlessly about the sitting-room. 'I mean to be up early to look through them before I pick up Fergus at the Pattersons' because I've simply got to know what they might say in advance.'

Katherine found extra blankets in a chest of drawers in the bedroom and they made up the settee.

'You're sure we can't swop?' she asked. 'I really don't mind the settee.'

'I'm not going to be here all the time,' Emma pointed out practically. 'It'll be much tidier if you sleep in the bed.'

They slept soundly, wakening in the morning to the sound of traffic outside their window instead of the plaintive bleating of sheep that greeted them in the glen.

'I'm going for the papers,' Emma called as she went out. 'You can put on the kettle and boil a couple of eggs.'

Katherine, who hadn't unpacked fully the night before, hung up two woollen dresses in the fitted wardrobe and put a change of underwear in one of the drawers. The rest could wait, she thought. She had laid hairbrushes, comb and make-up on the dressing-table top and put her shoes neatly beneath when the door bell rang.

'It's me,' said Emma from outside the main door. 'Can you let me in?'

Whom did she expect? Katherine pressed the door release with a wry smile. Charles?

'I forgot to take the keys.' Emma whirled past her into the living-room after depositing butter and a jar of marmalade on the kitchen bench. 'Listen to this! I quote: "Yesterday, at the Lovelle Gallery, a small exhibition of paintings drew me in with no great expectation of what I might find. Another mediocre collection was possibly my first reaction, but within minutes I was viewing the sort of work I've been searching for over the past five years. Here were landscapes and seascapes of tremendous power, with an individual depth and colouring to gladden the heart. No one who has even the least interest in art should fail to come here. The artist is completely unknown, so I doubt if he has ever exhibited his work before, otherwise we would have heard of him. Go to the Lovelle and see for yourself. These are paintings which will make their mark eventually. They are not great works of art, but they will hold their own in the galleries of the world in time."' Emma drew in a long, quivering breath. 'That will do for a start,' she decided, laying the newspaper aside. 'Now for the others!'

They went through three morning papers before they realised that the eggs had boiled dry and only one critic dismissed the exhibition as 'a tedious repetition of the expected', which made Emma's blood boil.

'What does *he* know about it?' she demanded angrily. 'If he's "never heard of Fergus Moreton", he will!'

Katherine was reading the final review over her shoulder, the eggs forgotten.

'It means we're going to be busy,' she said, 'and your faith in Fergus is vindicated.'

Emma's eyes glowed, and in that moment she looked beautiful.

'I knew he could do it,' she said quietly. 'Long ago I knew, but he wouldn't listen to me. Perhaps it took your enthusiasm to convince him,' she added generously. 'Whichever way, we have a celebration on our hands. What price a champagne lunch before we go back to Glassary?'

'Shouldn't we wait for results?' Katherine asked cautiously. 'Critics aren't always taken at their word.'

'You're remembering what I said yesterday,' Emma laughed, completely intoxicated by the reviews. 'But I feel success in my bones now.' She flourished the newspapers. 'This is unstinted praise. It will bring them in!'

Fergus had already seen the critics' verdict by the time they reached Morningside.

'We're early,' Emma announced, 'because we simply couldn't bear to wait!'

'It's encouraging,' he said modestly. 'More than encouraging, I suppose. I must confess I didn't expect to be praised so highly right away.'

'Well,' Emma said, 'this will be our busy day, but working hard is part of it. My mother says you never achieve anything unless you're willing to put your back into it, so here goes!'

They said goodbye to the Pattersons and drove quickly to the gallery.

'Doesn't everything look quite different this morning?' Emma said.

Her joy was so infectious that they had to laugh.

'By ten o'clock we're going to be swamped,' she predicted.

It was eleven before the public began to come in, squeezing through the narrow doorway to pay the small entrance fee which included a copy of the catalogue. Some of them were carrying morning newspapers; others were there to see exactly what was going on.

Katherine was kept far too busy to notice the individual viewer, but even without looking up from her task of parcelling Emma's sculptures she could hear what was being said. 'Wonderful!' 'Quite unique, if you ask me', 'A change, thank heaven, from the eternal green blob on a red background entitled "Sunrise" or "Sunset" or whatever one would like to suggest!' were the phrases she heard most frequently, and soon she was tying up small framed examples of Fergus's work which had been bought and paid for on the spot.

'I'm going back to the flat,' Emma announced at four o'clock. 'We must have some kind of celebration.'

Unsuspecting, Katherine handed over the keys.

'Don't be too long,' she said. 'Trade's booming!'

It was six o'clock before Emma returned.

'I had some shopping to do,' she explained enigmatically.

She was an entirely new person, gay and bright as she revelled in Fergus's success and the obvious change in him.

'If this goes on we're going to need help or Fergus will have to stay in Edinburgh,' she said, looking down the still busy gallery. 'That might be the best idea,' she added. 'He ought to savour his triumph to the full. Not that it's likely to give him a swollen head,' she hastened to explain, 'but he does deserve it. He's hoped for this moment for so long. Oh—look who's here!'

Katherine swung round to find Charles standing in the doorway.

'Chay!' Emma exclaimed, rushing forward to greet him. 'This is wonderful!' She relieved him of the large paper bag he was carrying. 'We didn't expect to see you. Can you get in?'

Charles stepped aside to let one of their customers out while Katherine stood watching, painfully aware of the turbulent beating of her heart. She had thought never to see Charles again, and here he was!

The last customer paid for the carving he had bought and went out. Emma closed the door with a deeply indrawn breath of satisfaction.

'Well, how about that?' she asked.

'It looks as if you've been most successful,' Charles said, shaking his brother by the hand. 'We're all going to tell you we knew it would happen, but congratulations, anyway. I've read the morning papers. You've evidently been discovered!'

He looked at Katherine at last, his eyes warm and friendly, thanking her for what she had done to help his brother find himself.

'It certainly calls for a celebration,' he said. 'I brought some champagne.'

'We'll have it in the flat,' Emma suggested mysteriously. 'You won't mind?'

He shook his head.

'Why should I? I only hope you were comfortable last night.' He was looking at Katherine again. 'I forgot to mention extra blankets.'

'We found them in the bedroom.' She was able to speak casually, although some of the warmth he had shown her was reflected in her eyes. 'The flat was so much nicer than being in an hotel.'

'I've set out some things.' Emma was still being mysterious. 'I thought it would be nicer than drinking warm champagne in the office!'

Fergus was wandering between the cubicles, assessing their success.

'I'll have to go back to Glassary for those other paintings,' he said. 'It's unbelievable!'

'If I'd phoned before I'd set out I could have brought them with me,' Charles acknowledged, 'but I'll take you back in the morning if Emma wants to stay.'

'Emma *has* to stay!' said Emma with a twinkle in her eye. 'I'll phone home and let them know.'

'Morag has already seen the reviews,' Charles told her. 'She's absolutely bursting with pride.'

Emma looked surprised.

'And I thought she might be resentful,' she said, 'because of the hotel. One never knows!'

They switched off the overhead lights, going out into the street to congregate in a talkative little group while Fergus locked the door.

'I never thought we'd do it,' he said when he joined them.

They drove to the flat in Katherine's car, Charles taking the wheel.

'Did you come across in the Rover?' Fergus asked.

Charles nodded.

'I parked it at the flat, and I've phoned the Pattersons to ask if they can put me up for a night.'

'I'm keeping you out of your own flat,' Katherine said. 'I could easily have gone to a hotel if I'd known.'

'It will only be for one night,' he answered. 'Don't feel too badly about it when you've done so much for Fergus in the meantime. The flat's a convenience I rarely use and it's better occupied.'

He pulled up in Heriot Row, finding a convenient parking place, and they walked along the pavement to the flat. Katherine produced the keys, handing them over to him to open the door. It was like coming home; coming back to a place of one's own after a busy, successful day!

Charles opened the flat door to a suggestion of well-being within. Someone had put flowers in the hall, leaving all the inner doors open so that the heat from the radiators could surge through and the light could come in from the windows. Emma, of course! This was what she had been doing during that stolen time in the afternoon when she had left the gallery. She had planned a celebration which would be a far more personal thing for Fergus than going to a restaurant.

In the living-room they found the table set out with convenience foods from a local delicatessen—prawns and stuffed olives and pâté, and cold meats with bowls of salad in between, and more flowers arranged in the centre. Emma had 'gone to town' in a big way, even finding glasses from somewhere in which to drink the champagne. There were only three glasses, and she said obligingly:

'I'll settle for a mug! We didn't expect you, Chay, but you're more than welcome!'

Charles drew the cork from one of the bottles he had brought.

'To your continuing success!' he said, holding up his glass as he looked across the table at his brother. 'And to your future happiness at the Stable House!'

'I think I value my future at the Stable House even more than my success,' said Fergus. 'Im hoping to make my home there when the time comes.'

Charles lowered his glass. He had been looking at Katherine, seeing the happiness in her eyes, and suddenly he turned away.

'Don't wait too long,' he murmured under his breath.

Because they had so much to talk about they lingered in the flat till midnight. They were tired, but neither Katherine nor Emma wanted to break up the party.

'When did you think of all this?' Katherine asked as they stood together for a moment.

'It came to me when I was thinking of food!' Emma's eyes were bright from drinking Charles's champagne. 'I couldn't settle for sausage-and-mash when we'd done so well. I've hidden my bottle of inferior hooch, by the way,' she added. 'It would have done nothing for us in comparison with Chay's champagne!'

'I think he looks—pensive,' Katherine said.

'Brooding over the past, do you mean? No, I don't think so,' Emma decided. 'Charles got over Deirdre a long time ago.'

The name struck at Katherine like a whiplash.

'Did she—plan the flat?' Her heart seemed to be beating close against her throat. 'Were they engaged to be married?'

'It's a long story,' Emma said. 'Ask me some other time.'

It was the wrong moment to ask about Charles's past, Katherine realised, and possibly Emma thought that she had no right to ask at all. It had been a wonderful evening, and if Charles had indeed looked thoughtful at times as he had glanced round him at the effort Emma had made it might be only natural in the circumstances. He had given the girl he loved a free hand to furnish the flat to her own taste, and if she had failed him in some way it was equally natural that he should see it now as the place it might have been. Emma's flowers and the set table and the warmth from the radiators now that the thick velvet curtains were drawn had made a difference.

When he was preparing to leave she asked him about Sandy.

'It was difficult to explain that he couldn't come with me,' he said. 'He was quite sure you would want to see him.'

'I found it hard to part with him.' She looked down at her clasped hands. 'Sandy and I were friends.'

'I think I recognised that when I first saw you together,' he said. 'Fergus will probably bring him through to the exhibition before you close.'

Fergus came across the room to put a friendly hand on his shoulder.

'High time we were on our way,' he suggested. 'Working girls have to get up early in the morning. I'll get back with the extra pictures as quickly as I can,' he assured Emma. 'Anything else you need from Glassary?'

'Just some fresh air!' Emma laughed. 'I'm not cut out for life as a shopkeeper.'

Katherine followed them to the door.

'I envy you the journey back to the glen,' she said impulsively. 'Perhaps I wasn't cut out for shop work, either.'

Charles looked at her, wondering about her, perhaps, as she stood on his doorstep bidding him goodnight. Did it remind him of that other flat in London, confirming his first opinion of her? Katherine turned away from the thought with a wry smile. It couldn't matter very much now, in any case, she thought, because after the exhibition closed they would go their separate ways. Without regret? The regret would be all on her side, she imagined as she turned back into the hall with its deep purple carpet and Emma's flowers making a brilliant splash of colour against the apple-green walls.

CHAPTER SEVEN

THE exhibition went from strength to strength and very soon Fergus had to persuade his customers to leave his pictures on the walls where possible so that there would be something to be seen.

There was a tremendous change in him as each day passed and the crowds continued to flock to the gallery. He was buoyant and eager, never tiring in his effort to please or explain, and when people were argumentative he bore with them; when they were kind he accepted their praise modestly, and when they were no more than indifferent he allowed them to waste his time with a happy smile. When Emma suggested that some of them only came in out of the rain, he laughed.

'There's plenty of room for everybody,' he said indulgently, 'and Kate can always present them with a catalogue for future reference!'

When they discussed his work more seriously, which they frequently did, he said earnestly:

'It makes me feel independent, Kate, for the first time since the accident. I can't tell you how much that means to me. My life is my own again. Not that I'll ever be able to repay Charles for all he's done, but I'm sure you know what I mean.'

They were often alone at the gallery when Emma had to return to the hotel to help her mother, and a firm friendship had developed between them which had really nothing to do with Sandy.

'I wish you'd come back to Glassary for a spell when this is over,' he said once. 'You really haven't got another job to go to right away.'

'I'll find one,' Katherine said, nearly choking on the words as she considered the inevitable ending of their friendship. 'There must be plenty to be had in Edinburgh or London.'

'London is very far away,' he said without pressing too hard for a decision.

When she was alone in the flat Katherine took the opportunity to tidy up. After the party they had stacked away china and glass, leaving only the essentials for a light meal in the evenings if they didn't want to go out to a restaurant, and mugs and bowls to hold their breakfast cereal. Emma would not be sleeping at the flat again because only four days remained until they had to hand over the gallery key to a new tenant and Katherine had offered to manage on her own until they closed.

Emma had folded her blankets on a chair in the bedroom, promising to put them away later, but they were still where she had left them and Katherine selected the deepest drawer in the chest which stood against the wall, thinking to find it empty, but it was half full of tissue paper and various odds and ends which Charles probably considered to be dispensable in a bachelor flat. It was still the best place for the blankets, however, and she started to gather the other things together to put them in one of the shallower drawers. There was a rubber hot-water bottle, an old pair of leather slippers and a silver photograph frame turned face down on the tissue paper as if it had been forgotten.

Picking it up, she knew herself suddenly reluctant to turn it over. If it was someone's photograph, long cherished by Charles, she had really no right to pry.

Handling it, she found the frame coming apart, the velvet back slipping as she tried to keep it in place and the portrait itself falling to the floor. It lay there on the deep purple pile of the carpet, face uppermost, and she knew that she had rarely seen such a beautiful girl before. Deeply penetrating eyes gazed up at her as if in amazement while the lovely mouth seemed to break into a smile. Smooth fair hair was drawn back from a high forehead with a little tortoiseshell comb and the pale, petal-smooth skin looked like silk. Only the bold, rounded signature in one corner looked hard. 'Deirdre,' she read, 'With love.'

Shaken by the sudden revelation that this was the girl Charles had wanted to marry, she picked up the pieces of the frame, trying to fit the photograph back into it while a dozen conflicting emotions struggled in her heart. It seemed that all the grief she had ever known had culminated in this moment, but there were no tears to wash it away. Deirdre, beloved of Charles, was no longer here, but the memory of her lingered. Their contact had scarred his life in some way, and the thought of it remained. The flat was the home he had prepared for her in Edinburgh, the complete antithesis to Glassary because she might have found it dull, and he could not bring himself to part with it.

The deep purple carpet was something Deirdre had chosen, and it was still there, dominating the entire flat. Only the smiling portrait had been hidden away.

Katherine put it back into the drawer where she had found it, covering it with the tissue paper, and found another store for Emma's blankets in the cupboard above the hot-water tank, but she couldn't banish the thought of Deirdre so easily. One day she might return, making Charles's life complete.

That could be why he kept the flat, hoping against hope that she would come.

Emma had promised to tell her about Deirdre, but now she didn't want to know. She was a coward in that respect, she told herself, although she had no hope of Charles ever loving her in return. Madly she had told him that she loved him, and he had not answered her. The hot colour of embarrassment rose in her cheeks as she thought about her confession, but there was no one there in the flat to see.

Perhaps it was to be expected that the last few days of the exhibition would be hectic, but she managed on her own easily enough. Now that she had gained some of the experience she needed she could discuss the catalogue knowledgeably enough even with the experts, and she was glad when people came back more than once. The curious ones wanted to know all about Fergus, where he came from and how long he had been painting, and Emma had her own coterie of admirers.

Once she caught a small boy stuffing a carved otter into his pocket, but he was so like Sandy that she found it hard to remonstrate with him, making him a present of the little model much to his mother's mortification.

'I'm always telling him he shouldn't *take* things,' she apologised, fumbling for her purse, 'but he doesn't seem to understand.'

'This time it's all right,' said Katherine, 'but I'll try to explain.'

She knelt down beside the child, admiring the otter as he held on to it with grim determination in his blue eyes.

'I'd like you to have it,' she said, 'but we must pay for it first. Will you come to the office till I find my purse?'

He exchanged a doubtful glance with his embarrassed mother.

'Go when you're told,' she said. 'The lady's being very kind.'

In the privacy of the office Katherine said very firmly:

'You won't do this again, will you? Everything has to be paid for, like Mummy pays for the groceries she picks up in the supermarket. They aren't free. You see, people have to make these things and it takes a long time, so we mustn't expect them for nothing.'

The boy looked at her with a dawning awareness in his blue eyes as she passed over the neatly-tied parcel.

'What's your name?' she asked.

'Sandy.'

Katherine's heart contracted with the well known pain as she led him back to the cubicle where his mother was waiting.

'I'm fair affronted,' the woman said. 'Could I give you something towards it, miss?'

It was painfully obvious to Katherine that she had 'just

come in out of the rain' and couldn't afford expensive sculptures.

'No. It's a gift. I know another Sandy who has plenty of animals to play with.'

The woman pulled the child away, remonstrating with him till they were safely outside, and Katherine went back to the office to make out a receipt. To keep the records straight, she told herself.

The final day of the exhibition dawned fine and clear. Emma had telephoned from the hotel the evening before to say that they would be in Edinburgh early to help with the tidying up and that they would be bringing Sandy with them.

'He's got this fixation about the Zoo,' she had explained, 'and Fergus thought he might be able to take him for a couple of hours before we finally packed up.'

So she was to see Sandy again, if not Charles!

Katherine was already tidying up in the office and marking off the unsold canvases which they would take back to Glassary with them. There weren't many left, and the fact was a source of encouragement for the future. She could see it all quite plainly: Fergus and Emma working hard at the Stable House, sharing their enthusiasm and their life, while Sandy grew up strong and affectionate beside them. The Stable House would be full of shared endeavour and duplicated love, while at Glassary—At Glassary?

She busied herself with her tasks, not troubling to eat lunch because she was suddenly busy again. The inevitable end of the exhibition rush was upon her.

Emma had phoned earlier to say they were in Edinburgh and she had pressed her to spend some of the time with Fergus and Sandy at the Zoo.

'Go with them,' she had said. 'You won't be wasting time. Think of all the other animals you'll see there!'

'Are you sure?' Emma had asked with a note of excitement in her voice. 'You'll be on your own.'

'I'll cope,' Katherine had assured her. 'We're not as

busy as we were yesterday, and you can help me with the packing when you eventually get here.'

She had honestly not expected to be so busy, but selling paintings was a leisurely business compared to some and she was able to satisfy everybody.

When the crowd was thickest around three o'clock she had the disconcerting sensation of being watched, but she was able to dismiss it because she hadn't much time for impressions during these last few hours, but when the crowd thinned again she became aware of a girl in a long green coat standing near the door. She seemed to be examining the painting on the easel which Fergus had placed as a single attraction in the window to draw the crowd, and something about her seemed vaguely familiar.

When she went out at the door a moment or two later she walked briskly away.

She was back again, however, when the gallery cleared, standing beside one of the display tables pretending to examine one of Emma's sculptures, and when she looked up Katherine gasped.

'Coralie!' she exclaimed. 'What are you doing here?'

'I'm curious, for one thing.' Coralie came towards her. 'Though I didn't expect to find you behind the shop counter! I'm intrigued, of course,' she added with the brief laugh Katherine remembered so well. 'Is it Fergus you plan to marry, or Charles?'

Katherine ignored both laugh and question.

'What are you doing in Edinburgh?' she demanded, suddenly angry because she was thinking of all this might mean to Fergus and Emma if Fergus had never really forgotten his ex-wife.

'I was going to ask the same question.' Coralie still looked faintly amused although her expression had hardened. 'You were at Glassary when you phoned me in London. The fact gave me the faintest of shocks when Mendell told me. He's Stephanie's boy-friend, by the way, and he happened to be in the flat when you rang,' she added. 'You hadn't met, but he did say you'd phoned twice.'

'I had to let you know about Sandy,' Katherine explained, trying to curb her anger, 'and I had to tell you about your sister. She wasn't at Beck Cottage when we got there.'

Coralie's eyes narrowed.

'So you took the law into your own hands and went on to Glassary,' she suggested.

'Not quite.' Vividly Katherine was remembering the sequence of events which had taken her to Charles's kingdom. 'When I was almost at Kendal I thought I was being followed. It was Charles Moreton—but perhaps you won't be too surprised at that.'

'Not really.' Coralie was watching her closely. 'I knew he was in London, you see, and it wasn't too difficult to guess that he was looking for me.'

Katherine's accusing gaze met hers.

'Because you weren't playing fair?' she suggested. 'Sandy should have been returned to his father after his holiday with you in London. It wasn't Fergus who was kidnapping Sandy, it was you.'

Coralie shrugged.

'Does it really matter?' she asked. 'You needn't have become so—involved.'

'But I was involved, right from the start,' Katherine pointed out. 'You lied to me, Coralie. If you'd told me the truth I would never have promised to help you.'

Coralie looked about her.

'Aren't we being a bit aggressive?' she suggested. 'No harm has been done, as far as I can see.' Her eyes narrowed a little. 'Or is that it? Has your unexpected visit to Glassary given you ideas?'

'What I think about Glassary has nothing to do with it,' said Katherine under her breath. 'It's now that matters. Sandy and his father are here, in Edinburgh—with Emma Falkland.'

'Good heavens! Emma?' Coralie exclaimed. 'She was always crazy about him, of course, but it's most amusing, all the same. When I saw their exhibition advertised I don't think I was greatly surprised, but I would never have imagined this. Where are they, since they're not exactly helping to sell their wares?'

'They've taken Sandy to the Zoo.' Instantly Katherine wondered if she should have revealed the fact. 'They'll be here shortly.'

'And you don't think I should be waiting for them on the doorstep?'

Katherine didn't hesitate.

'No,' she said, 'I don't think you should do anything so dramatic. I think you should give yourself more time to think things over.'

'To think about my former marriage, do you mean?' Coralie picked up one of Emma's fragile sculptures, her blue eyes almost caressing it. 'She's making the most of her talent, isn't she? Emma, I mean. I suppose Sandy has dozens of these little animals.'

'It's natural enough,' Katherine pointed out. 'He watches Emma making them.'

'And they're all deliriously happy together,' Coralie concluded. 'This takes a lot of accepting.'

'Coralie,' Katherine appealed, 'don't make a hasty decision. If you're not able to look after Sandy—if you're going to be travelling all over the world—wouldn't it be better to leave things as they are?'

Coralie's eyes glittered.

'I suppose I want to go to Glassary,' she admitted, 'but I'm frantically busy. It's all happening for me now, Kate! I had a tremendous success in New York with my designs and now I'll be working here in Edinburgh for the Festival doing the scenery for a new play.'

'But that's not till August,' Katherine pointed out as she glanced towards the door.

'August isn't so far away,' Coralie declared. 'We're making contact now and I have to be on the spot for a while. It won't bring in a fortune, but it's an amazing feather in my cap for future reference.'

'Do you mean to go to Glassary?' Katherine asked.

'Why not? I want to see my child.'

Coralie was still looking about her, assessing the quality of her ex-husband's success.

'Is that quite fair?' Katherine asked slowly. 'Fergus has never refused you when you wanted to see Sandy, but he has custody under the law. Oh, I know how difficult all this must be for you,' she rushed on, 'wanting Sandy so much, but can you truthfully say he'll be better with you than at Glassary, where he belongs?'

'You're speaking on Charles's behalf, aren't you?' Coralie smiled. 'You know he will make Sandy his heir because he won't marry. Not after Deirdre. Ah! I see you know about her,' she added when Katherine looked away to hide the hurt in her eyes. 'She was Charles's one and only love, you know. "First love, deepest love," and all that sort of thing, never to be forgotten by a man like Charles.'

'I know he must have been very much in love with her,' Katherine said quietly, 'but we're talking about Sandy.'

Coralie assessed her for a moment.

'You really do fancy Charles, don't you?' she said. 'Poor Kate! You haven't a ghost of a chance. "Ghost" could be the operative word,' she added cruelly. 'Charles seems to be haunted by the past.'

'I don't want to discuss Charles!' Katherine protested. 'It's not my affair.'

'It is if you think he might notice you in future,' Coralie pointed out. 'The facts are not all that dramatic, really. Deirdre was one of those people who could pull the wool over anyone's eyes, and she did it with Charles because he trusted her implicitly. They became engaged and started to furnish a flat here, in Edinburgh. Perhaps I should say Deirdre started to furnish it, because everything was just as she wanted it—the best she could buy—while all the time there was someone else in the background. He was working abroad and she never thought he'd come back because they had parted in anger, but he did return and she married him within a week. It was as simple as that, and it's happening all the time nowadays, but can you imagine what it would do to Charles? He wanted nothing more to do with marriage after that, so he settled a lot of money on my son.'

'You told me that was why Fergus wanted Sandy back,' Katherine reminded her, 'but I know that isn't true. It was you who was interested in the money.'

Coralie shrugged.

'I had a right to some of it,' she declared. 'Now it doesn't matter so much. I can earn more than enough to keep myself and I won't be dependent on Charles's bounty from now on.' The harsh satisfaction in her voice made her seem even harder than Katherine imagined. 'He never really accepted me at Glassary, but I was his brother's wife and Sandy's mother and I was the necessary evil as far as the estate was concerned. We didn't get on together and probably he was glad when Fergus and I parted company.'

'But, Coralie, that's all over now,' Katherine protested. 'You left because you wanted a career.'

'And I can't have my cake and eat it! Is that what you're trying to say, Kate?'

'I've no right to preach to you, but my main concern is for Sandy,' Katherine said. 'He's so happy at the Stable House and very soon Fergus will be able to have him there for good. He's no longer a complete invalid, and now he has both an incentive to succeed and the means to do it.'

'And Emma, you forgot to say!'

'I don't know about Emma,' Katherine was forced to admit, 'but if they did marry I know she'd be good for Sandy.'

'Poor Emma!' Coralie said pityingly. 'She was always hopelessly in love with Fergus even before I came on the scene, I believe.'

'Well, you're not "on the scene" any more,' Katherine

said sharply. 'Give them a chance, since you *do* mean to go on with your career.'

Coralie prowled into the next cubicle.

'I had no idea Fergus was this much of a genius,' she mused. 'It must be very satisfying for him.' She turned to look at Katherine. 'How did you become so heavily involved?'

'My car broke down on my way to the Trossachs,' Katherine explained almost reluctantly. 'That was my original destination, if you remember, before I agreed to help you. When your sister wasn't at Beck Cottage I could only take Sandy with me since I couldn't get in touch with you in London, to put you in the picture. Oddly enough, I broke down near Glassary—or at least near the Falklands' hotel.' She knew that she was deliberately glossing over Charles's part in her adventure because it wasn't going to make any difference now. 'We stayed at the hotel that night and went on to Glassary the following morning. At least Sandy was safe there.'

'Did Charles invite you to stay?' Coralie asked curiously. 'Or was it Fergus?'

'There wasn't much choice. My car broke down and Charles had it towed to the nearest garage, but it took over a week to get the necessary part to mend it.'

'So you were quite some time at Glassary?' Coralie mused. 'What did you do with yourself, apart from falling in love with Charles?'

Katherine bit her lip.

'There was quite a lot to do even before the exhibition came along,' she said. 'I had the use of an old bicycle, and Sandy rode his pony about the glen and learned to fish in the loch. The days seemed to fly past before we were aware of them going because there was so much to do.'

'And whose idea was the exhibition?' Coralie wanted to know.

'Emma's, I think. She saw that it would be a wonderful chance for Fergus to regain his former confidence if it succeeded.'

'Is he still confined to a wheelchair?' Coralie asked idly. 'That was the part I hated most, seeing him just sitting there with time slipping through his fingers and both our lives going to waste.'

'Surely he must have been painting his pictures even then?' Katherine protested. 'That wasn't exactly wasting time.'

'Oh, yes, his pictures!' Coralie shrugged. 'They cut me out, too. He had always painted, but after the accident, when he got back the use of his hands, they were an obsession with him. He would sit all day with an easel in front of him just staring at the scenery and I was supposed to sit with him and carry half the load. Of course, there was Sandy,' she added reminiscently, 'but Mrs Stevas took over even when he was a baby and I was expected to wheel my husband around instead of the pram.'

Katherine drew in a deep breath.

'I'm sure it must have been—frustrating,' she said, 'but everyone would be trying to help. It could have worked out in the end.'

Coralie looked round at her.

'For you, perhaps,' she said, 'but not for me. I wanted my own life and I wanted my career. I think I realised how much I needed my freedom even before Sandy was born,' she added harshly. 'I felt trapped in a cocoon of ugliness all the time and I knew I would never have another child even though this wasn't the heir everyone wanted. Fergus accepted that, so I don't think he was too surprised when everything ended between us. Once he got the electric wheelchair he was more or less able to get about on his own and I was free to go.'

'Oh, don't make it sound so matter-of-fact!' Katherine protested inwardly, knowing how deeply Fergus had been hurt. Marriages aren't ended so easily.

'What's he like now?' Coralie demanded.

'He gets about without the chair whenever he can,' Katherine explained, 'although he still has to use a stick. It's been a kind of miracle that he's able to walk again.'

'It wasn't expected,' Coralie mused. 'There was very little hope in the beginning. Maybe Emma Falkland made the difference,' she laughed. 'She certainly worked hard at it. Are they going to marry?'

'I don't know.'

Katherine's breath caught in her throat when she thought of what Coralie's return might mean to Emma if she planned to go back to Glassary for good in spite of all she had said about her career, and hidden at the back of her mind was the thought that Fergus might still be half in love with his former wife.

At that moment her thought was to get Coralie out of the gallery before Emma and Fergus came in with Sandy.

'Where are you staying?' Coralie asked. 'I'm looking for somewhere to lay my head for a day or two.'

'At the flat.'

'Charles's flat?' Coralie was obviously taken aback. 'You couldn't surprise me more,' she admitted. 'Did he offer or did you ask?'

'You could hardly expect me to ask!' A customer came in and Katherine was able to turn away, hoping that Coralie would go. 'You'll have to excuse me.'

'Business first!' Coralie agreed lightly, but she did not go, lingering among the exhibits of Emma's sculptures till Emma herself came to the door.

Katherine saw her first and Emma had obviously recognised Coralie. All the healthy colour had drained out of her cheeks as she stood, ashen-faced, just inside the door looking as if she couldn't move.

'Excuse me!' Katherine left her customer to inspect the pictures. 'I know you'd like to look around.'

Emma was still standing beside the door, but she pulled herself together as Katherine approached, trying to smile.

'I left Sandy and his father at the Zoo,' she said through parched lips. 'I thought you might need help.'

Katherine tried to place herself between her and the

cubicle where Coralie was still examining her sculpture.

'We'll have some tea,' she said, 'in the office.'

Emma shook her head.

'It's no use, Kate,' she said. 'I had a feeling this would happen, sooner or later. The only thing I'm glad about is that Fergus didn't come back with me to be—surprised like this.'

She walked towards the cubicle and Coralie looked up and smiled.

'A day of meetings!' she remarked glibly. 'I was more than surprised to see Katherine here, of course, but I did expect to see you and—possibly—Fergus.'

'Is that why you came to Edinburgh?' Emma asked.

'Not really.' Coralie was looking at her intently, recognising her distress. 'But I did see your advertisement in the papers as soon as I arrived and curiosity did the rest! I had to come and see for myself exactly what was going on.'

Emma turned to look about her at all the signs of her success—hers and Fergus's.

'We used to talk about having an exhibition at Glassary, if you remember,' she said. 'It hasn't just materialised out of the blue.'

'But it did seem impossible at one time,' Coralie pointed out. 'Now I hear that Fergus is on his feet again.'

'Yes. He'll never be able to walk as well as he did, but he's a whole man again in many ways. This success has meant a lot to him. Please don't try to rob him of his newly-found peace of mind.'

Emma's sombre violet eyes were fixed relentlessly on the blue ones which had mocked her when she had first come in and her lips had regained their habitual firmness.

'You're asking me to step aside,' Coralie said incredulously. 'Don't you think that's a little dangerous?'

'I'm not asking you to do anything for me,' Emma said quietly. 'It's Fergus and Sandy I'm thinking about. If you don't mean to go back to Glassary permanently you'll upset them both. Sandy has settled in now; he's happy and so is Fergus. Give them a chance.'

'You're speaking for yourself, too,' Coralie smiled. 'Arguing your own cause because you've always been in love with Fergus.'

Emma didn't contradict her. Instead she went on into the office, ostensibly to make the tea.

'Poor Emma!' Coralie said with mock pity. 'She was always hopelessly infatuated with my ex-husband and I dare say me turning up like this has been a great shock to her. She probably had everything worked out to her own satisfaction—the exhibition, Fergus's returning pride and, no doubt, Sandy into the bargain.'

'At least there's nothing sham about her affection for Sandy,' said Katherine. 'I hope you're not going to take him away from Glassary again.'

Surprisingly Coralie looked indecisive.

'I'm not sure what I'm going to do,' she admitted, unsure for the first time in her life. 'I want Sandy—who wouldn't?—but I can't give him a secure home at present. Not while I'm still clawing my way to the top. I'm determined to get there, so that's about it,' she added. 'Fergus has to agree to let me see Sandy from time to time. That's in law, but I suppose I could demand more.' The blue eyes searched Katherine's. 'What are you going to do after the exhibition is over? Are you going back to Glassary?'

Katherine shook her head.

'I'll be looking for a job,' she said.

'In Edinburgh? We could meet occasionally while I'm here, in that case,' Coralie suggested.

'No, Coralie!' Katherine was adamant. 'Our last meeting caused me a lot of pain. You lied to me; you said Fergus was trying to kidnap Sandy and I believed you when it wasn't true. It was you who wanted him then, as perhaps you do now, for an extremely selfish reason, but Charles will never forgive me for my part in that deception.'

'So it *is* Charles!' Coralie said with quick perception. 'Well, well, well!'

When she had gone Katherine made her way back to the office past the happily absorbed customers who were still examining Fergus's paintings. Emma was standing beside the desk staring down unseeingly at the clutter of bills and orders which still littered it.

'I shouldn't have said my piece,' she acknowledged. 'I told her literally to stay away from Glassary when I had absolutely no right.'

'You were taken by surprise.'

'I don't think so.' Emma collected some bills. 'I had a feeling Coralie would turn up if only to prove she had still some sort of hold on Fergus. She's quite sure he could never really get over her.'

'And has he?'

'I thought so.' Emma could not meet her eyes. 'I thought this success we've had together had made a difference, but the one thing I couldn't bear is to see him suffering all over again. Because, you see, I don't think Coralie really wants him for keeps.'

'She doesn't know what she wants!' Katherine rapped out angrily. 'She was ready to ditch Sandy and everything else for her career and I don't think she's really changed. I think she's intrigued by a situation that's got beyond her and she doesn't know what to do.'

'It's what I have to do that worries me,' said Emma, looking through the glass partition which separated the office from the gallery proper. 'I'd willingly give up all this to make Fergus happy.'

'And undo everything you've already achieved!'

'If I thought he was still in love with her, that he could carry on with her help, I'd—make myself scarce,' Emma said.

'I can't see Coralie going back to Glassary for good, if that's what you mean,' said Katherine. 'She'd wilt there in a couple of months pining for what she believed she'd lost.'

'I wish I could be sure.' Emma was watching the door for Fergus's return. 'I'm glad they didn't meet before he knew she was in Edinburgh,' she said. 'It can be such a shock coming on someone you least expect when you're suddenly so sure of the future. I'll tell Fergus, of course, when we're alone,' she added. 'He has a right to know that Coralie is here, but we don't have to upset Sandy needlessly.' She pushed the half-resolved problem away from her. 'What are we going to do about the flat?' she asked. 'Can you tidy up on your own if I go back to the hotel with Sandy and Fergus? Charles said not to rush; you were welcome to stay there as long as you liked till you fixed up another job.'

Katherine turned her back.

'I can't go on accepting his hospitality for ever,' she said unevenly. 'It was different when I was working here for Fergus, but after this weekend there won't be any reason to stay on.'

'No,' said Emma, 'if you feel obliged, but I don't think you should. Charles has always been determined to do the best he can for Fergus, and you were more than helpful in that respect.'

She hesitated, as if she was about to impart a further confidence, and then she seemed to think better of the impulse as Sandy came bounding in at the main door followed by his father.

'I've been to the Zoo an' I've seen a elephant an' a camel an' a tiger an' a big brown bear an' a jag'ar an' a lot of goats an' birds an' ducks, like at Glassary!' he announced excitedly. 'An' there was snakes an' parrots an' things——'

'Take a deep breath!' Emma advised, lifting him into her arms. 'Otherwise you'll go off pop! Did you see the lions?' She kissed his cheek.

'Yes, I saw two lions an' they had two baby lions as well. They were sittin' on some rocks, but one lion was walking up and down, watching everybody. I think he didn't like people staring at his babies.'

'I guess not.' Emma was looking at Fergus. 'There's quite a lot to pack if we're going to take everything back with us,' she pointed out. 'More than we can cope with in the Mini, I'm afraid.'

Fergus looked at Katherine.

'Kate could bring the rest,' he suggested. 'I've already asked her to come back to the glen for a few days.'

'I'll be looking for a job,' Katherine reminded him, although her pulses were already racing at the thought of the glen.

'Come, all the same,' he said.

'I'll get the pictures ready, anyway,' she promised, confused because it was her dearest wish to return to Glassary, but not like this. Not on Fergus's invitation only.

There were still a few people in the gallery, the inevitable stragglers who came in late and lingered after closing time pretending a profound interest but not buying. Emma glanced at her watch.

'If we're going to make the glen before bedtime,' she said, looking in Sandy's direction, 'I think we should be on our way. You're quite sure you can manage by yourself?' she asked Katherine once more.

'Once this lot make up their minds to go it won't take me very long to clear up,' Katherine assured her. 'I'll come back for the remainder of the pictures in the morning,' she added, 'and leave them at the flat.'

'Bring them to Glassary,' Fergus insisted. 'You can't possibly want to look for another job right away.'

'I'll see,' she told him vaguely.

'We'll give you till Tuesday,' he said, 'and if you don't turn up by then we'll come and fetch you.'

It was the decision she should have made for herself, Katherine thought, to let them come back for the pictures and then make some excuse for not going to Glassary.

Her heart felt as cold as ice as she watched them pack most of the unsold canvases in the boot before they turned to help Sandy into the car. He was still excited by his busy day and she stooped to kiss him on the cheek as they parted.

'Take care of the animals,' she said huskily. 'Especially Fudge.'

'Uncle Charles has mended your bike,' he remembered. 'It's all ready for you to ride again.'

She hugged him close to hide the tears which gathered in her eyes.

'Goodbye, darling,' she said under her breath.

'Remember what I said.' Fergus got in beside Emma when he had finally locked the boot. 'Tuesday—or else!'

'I'll remember.'

She stood in the doorway, watching them go, seeing Sandy's fair head through the back window until the Mini turned a corner and was lost to her for ever.

I won't go, she thought. I couldn't bear the pain of going back to the glen, not even to the hotel.

CHAPTER EIGHT

It wasn't difficult to clear the gallery, but she decided to leave the remainder of the paintings there overnight and collect them the following day. Then she would take them to the flat and hand the keys over to the caretaker and that would be that. It would be the end of a happy chapter in her life when she had come to know Fergus and Emma intimately while they worked together for the common good, and certainly the exhibition had been that for Fergus, at least. The change in him had been miraculous and the thought of Coralie upsetting it all was too much to contemplate, but Coralie was an unstable sort of person, given to sudden impulses, which might easily complicate the situation once again. The half-promise she had made had very little substance behind it, and even as she had talked of 'sharing' Sandy under the terms of the law she had been doubtful about the actual result. She was still 'clawing her way to the top', as she had put it so succinctly, and she meant to give her undivided attention to that end. She could, however, make it impossible for Sandy to settle and Fergus to forget her completely. She could still spoil his life—and Emma's—by being there and wanting to dominate the scene by asserting her rights. Yet, if she succeeded in her career, if her life became full and satisfying elsewhere, it was doubtful if she would ever want to see Glassary again.

When she had locked the canvases in the office, Katherine closed the gallery door and walked slowly along the almost deserted streets to where she had parked her car. Edinburgh in this evening hour was an enchanted place, with the old houses looking down at her on either side and the shadowy vennels guarding their secrets as she passed. The sun had set towards the west, leaving haunting shadows among the gabled roofs and slants of yellow light at the corners where the tall buildings came closely together like whispering neighbours, their heads almost touching as they gossiped together at the ending of another day. Yet she could not feel the warmth of friendship nor the happiness of belonging. She had never felt so alone in all her life as when the Mini had turned the corner and disappeared from view.

As she opened the door of her car it seemed to be the ending of a chapter which could never be re-written, however hard she tried. The initial mistake she had made in trusting Coralie implicitly had brought her confusion and heartache, but it had also brought her companionship and love. She would never forget Emma and Fergus and Sandy, who had left a bright warmth in her heart, just as she could never forget Charles, who must still hold her in absolute contempt. So much so that he must only be glad that she would never return to the glen.

There was very little to do when she reached the flat because she had decided to tidy up finally on the Monday morning. After that she would leave, phoning through to Emma at the hotel to tell her what she had done. The paintings would be safe enough at the flat until someone could come to Edinburgh to collect them.

All next day she wondered about Glassary, thinking that the routine would be very much the same as it had always been; seeing Sandy riding down to the Stable House on his pony or sitting bolt upright on Fergus's knee while the electric wheelchair careered down the slope towards the loch; seeing Fergus preparing a new canvas for his brush while he discussed it with Emma, or even showing it to Charles. There would be the boat on the loch lying beside the wooden jetty with the oars ready, and the ducks congregating among the reeds, and high up against the rugged contours of the mountains there would be a kestrel or a buzzard hovering above the moor to plummet in a magnificent aerial dive when it found its prey.

Because it was a day for heights she climbed to the top of Arthur's Seat to look down on the broad estuary of the Forth and beyond the water to the green Ochils standing in a bright half-circle, shutting out the wind from the north. Edinburgh lay at her feet, its undoubted magic casting its spell until she knew that she would stay there for good or ill. This lovely northern capital with its grey towers and battlemented castle standing high on its ancient rock had bewitched her, and she would look for a job here. London, in comparison, seemed very far away.

Her decision made, she scanned an old issue of *The Scotsman* to assess the situation as it would affect her and decided that her chances were good. In the morning she would ring an agency, leaving her credentials with them for reference.

It occurred to her, then, to phone Emma at the hotel, telling her that she would leave the paintings at the flat for Fergus to collect when he was next in Edinburgh. There was a long pause before Emma answered.

'I think you're wrong,' she said slowly, 'avoiding Glassary like this. I think you ought to come back to the glen even if it's only to say goodbye.'

'I've already said my goodbyes.' Katherine almost choked on the words. 'I couldn't bear to do it all over again, especially if I met Charles.'

'I guess that would be inevitable if you went to Glassary,' Emma agreed, 'but why not come here and take a chance?'

'Later, perhaps,' said Katherine. 'I'll look for a job, Emma, and then I'll contact you again.'

'I hope you will,' Emma said doubtfully, 'but I warn you that Fergus might not take "no" for an answer. He's very grateful for your help, Kate. We all are, and we'll be terribly disappointed if you cut adrift.'

'I won't do that,' Katherine whispered. 'Honestly. I'll be in touch when I've settled in and perhaps we can meet when you come to Edinburgh.'

'You're still at the flat, of course?' Emma asked.

'Till tomorrow. Then I mean to look for a quiet hotel where I can stay for a while until I land a suitable job. Wish me luck!' she added as lightly as she could.

Emma said: 'Of course I wish you luck, but not while you're being stupid and renouncing all your friends. You've done so much for us, Kate, we simply *have* to care about you. Fergus isn't going to be at all pleased when he hears your decision.'

Katherine put down the receiver, her vision blurred by the tears she could no longer hold in check. They had become friends in the shortest space of time because Emma and Fergus had judged her impartially, apart from Coralie, but Charles had seen her as just another lightweight character like his sister-in-law and his former fiancée, and that alone would keep her from returning to the glen.

In the morning she packed her suitcase, leaving it just inside the door beside the paintings she had collected from the gallery the evening before. The view of the glen she had bought for herself was still unwrapped and she stood looking at it for one tender moment before she found the corrugated cardboard and brown paper in which to protect it against damage until she found a place for it on the wall of some other flat or even in a bed-sitter somewhere in the suburbs.

Even after she had dusted the living-room and smoothed out the cushions for the last time it was still only eleven o'clock. She had nearly a whole day before her, the first of many lonely days. They would fall into a pattern in the end when she eventually found work, but it would be a pattern far removed from Glassary.

The door bell rang, jolting her thoughts back to the present, although she could not imagine whom it might be. Wildly she thought of Charles, her pulses racing for a moment, but when she lifted the receiver it was a woman's voice that answered.

'It's Coralie,' she said. 'Can you let me in?'

Katherine's first impulse was to refuse, to say 'no' because Coralie had caused so much trouble in the past, and then, almost automatically, she pressed the button which released the lock on the main door.

She was standing at the entrance to the flat when Coralie came up the stairs, and she saw instantly that her visitor had spent a restless night.

'I have to talk to you,' Coralie said, passing her as if she had expected to be kept standing on the landing. 'I've got a lot to say.'

'If it's about Sandy,' said Katherine, 'surely you've said it all?'

Coralie closed the door behind her.

'Not quite. I've taken nearly two days to think about it and now I've made my decision.' She walked into the tidy living-room. 'Are you leaving?' she asked.

'I can't stay here indefinitely now that the exhibition is over,' Katherine pointed out. 'Emma and I had the use of the flat while we were working at the gallery, but I can't expect Charles to go on accommodating me for ever.'

'Why not?' Coralie's eyes were brilliant. 'I could make this place look entirely different, given a chance,' she decided. 'I'd do away with this atrocious purple carpet, for a start, and change the wallpaper to liven things up a bit. Then I'd have different curtains and new furniture and plenty of side tables to reduce the space. I could do it over for Charles if he did want to let it.'

'I don't think he does,' Katherine said firmly, 'and I wouldn't ask, if I were you. What did you come to say to me?'

Coralie's enthusiasm died in her eyes as she met the challenge. She was no longer the effervescent designer, but a rather sad person who had come to a reluctant conclusion about her future.

'Could we have some coffee or something?' she asked plaintively. 'I have to talk.'

Katherine went towards the kitchen where everything had been washed and stacked away.

'I was going out to look for a hotel,' she explained. 'I won't be staying here tonight.'

'Surely a cup of coffee can't be too great a problem,' Coralie suggested, following her through. 'I'll help wash up afterwards, if you like.'

'Two mugs won't take much washing.' In the face of her visitor's obvious distress Katherine felt suddenly churlish. 'I'm sorry! I should have offered,' she apologised, 'but there isn't much to eat.'

'I don't eat in the middle of the morning,' Coralie said. 'I have to watch my figure, especially now that I'm going places and doing things. I've got that job I told you about, by the way,' she added, 'and the promise of a follow-up if I can go to Rome immediately afterwards. My designs are taking off in a big way.' Her blue eyes glittered. 'Success attracts success, as the saying goes!'

'I expect it does,' Katherine allowed, 'but that's not what you came to discuss, is it?'

Coralie spooned instant coffee powder into the jug she had found.

'No, it isn't,' she admitted. 'I don't know why I have to tell you, unless it's because you were so fond of Sandy.'

Katherine turned to look at her in the full light from the kitchen window. All the brilliant anticipation of a successful future had faded from Coralie's eyes and she looked lost. She was so like a bewildered Sandy in that moment that Katherine's heart seemed to turn over, and then she said:

'I guess I'm an essentially selfish person, Kate, but I've thought very carefully about the future now.' She carried the coffee jug into the living-room. 'You see, I hung around after I came to the gallery on Saturday afternoon intending to come back when Fergus had returned with Sandy. I *did* come back,' she added, 'and I was in one of the cubicles looking at Fergus's paintings when they arrived. I saw you all together then for the first time. I saw Sandy's joy and security and I knew I could never match it. I could never give him what he had at Glassary by right.' Her voice faltered as she looked through the window at the trees in the gardens across the road. 'I can hardly expect you to believe me,' she said, 'because it's the toughest decision I've ever made, but I *do* mean to put Sandy's interests first.'

Surprise and incredulity were both mirrored in Katherine's eyes, and suddenly she found herself wishing that Coralie hadn't told her about the wonderful chance she had been offered in Rome, about the amazing, continuing success of her career which seemed to be bounding forward by the hour. It made her decision about Sandy seem far too easy, her desire to do what was right for him ring slightly hollow even as she spoke.

'You're not saying very much,' Coralie challenged, sipping her coffee. 'Perhaps you don't believe what I've just said?'

'I want to believe you, Coralie, and I think I can understand how difficult it's been for you to decide,' Katherine said with genuine sympathy, 'but it would do more damage if you eventually went back on your word.'

'I'm not likely to do that.' Coralie drew a deep breath. 'I've thought everything out in the minutest detail, and even if I had Sandy I couldn't trail him all over the world in pursuit of my career. I had a decision to make. A terrible decision,' she added, her eyes suddenly beseeching in their evident sincerity about that, at least. 'It wasn't easy.'

Katherine's heart was suddenly touched by pity.

'I'm sure it wasn't,' she said, 'and I don't think Fergus or Emma will ever want to shut you out completely. There'll always be room for you in Sandy's life.'

'You speak of them together.' The blue eyes were sharply inquisitive. 'Will Fergus marry Emma?'

'Eventually, I think. They have so much in common,' Katherine pointed out.

Coralie nodded.

'That's what it's all about, isn't it?' she said. 'Having things in common, not wanting to rush off at a tangent to live your own life the way you want to. It's what's known as "togetherness" in the modern jargon, isn't it? Being a single unit instead of two individual personalities pulling in the opposite direction all the time. Fergus and I never had it,' she concluded. 'We should never have married.'

Katherine crossed to her side, her coffee mug still in her hand.

'It isn't easy,' she said, 'working all these things out, and when you're in love it doesn't seem to matter.'

'I thought I was in love in the beginning,' Coralie mused, 'until my life began to seem empty. It seemed empty long before Sandy was born, but he was the answer for a while, and then, after the accident, I knew. I could see all my future stretching before me with nothing done, and I couldn't bear to look at Fergus tied to a wheelchair for the rest of our lives together. You think that despicable, don't you, but it was how it was. I was twenty-four years of age and my life was over.'

'It needn't have been,' Katherine said quietly, 'but even that has to be a shared decision. How long will you stay in Edinburgh?' she asked to dispel the tension between them.

'For two weeks this time.' Coralie hesitated. 'Maybe I could see you once you're settled in somewhere,' she added unexpectedly. 'We'll both be tackling something new.'

The plea was for companionship and understanding while she needed it.

'You'll be far too busy,' Katherine pointed out, 'once you get fully into your stride.'

'Perhaps you're right.' Coralie was still gazing out of the window. 'Are you expecting a visitor?' she asked.

'No.' Katherine turned to look through the window. 'It will be for one of the other flats.'

A taxi had pulled up at the kerbside and a tall man in a tweed suit was getting out.

'It's Charles!' Coralie exclaimed.

Katherine stood looking down into Heriot Row, every pulse in her body throbbing as she watched the man she loved paying off the taxi before he walked briskly across the pavement towards the main door. Charles! Her heart cried wildly. Charles, why have you come?

Coralie moved at her elbow, making her realise how awkward the situation could prove to be. If Charles found Coralie visiting her he would surely think that they were still the best of friends.

Coralie laughed at her obvious concern.

'What do you want me to do?' she asked in her usual flippant manner. 'Hide in a convenient wardrobe?'

Katherine moved towards the door as the street bell rang.

'There's no need for anything so dramatic,' she said. 'Charles may only be coming to take away the paintings.'

In spite of her outward calm her hand was shaking as she lifted the receiver.

'May I come up?' Charles asked.

Her heart sank a little as she pressed the door release.

'Yes, please do,' she said.

Going through the hall to open the door she could not think what to say to him. To try to explain away Coralie's visit would only be to suggest that it mattered to him, and she didn't think it did, except perhaps where Sandy and Fergus were concerned. He had already made his decision about Coralie and also about herself, although he had been kind about the flat.

When she opened the door he looked immediately at the stacked paintings propped against the wall and her suitcase standing beside them, ready for her departure.

'Why did you change your mind about coming to Glassary?' he asked. 'You can't possibly have got another job right away.'

She swallowed hard.

'Edinburgh seemed the best place to look for one,' she said, following him into the living-room where Coralie was waiting.

'Hullo!' she greeted him lightly. 'Fancy our meeting! How are you, Charles, after all this time? You look just the same,' she ran on, not at all abashed by the situation, 'but that's probably the glen's amazing air!'

For a moment Charles looked angry.

'You didn't find it particularly invigorating while you lived there,' he reminded her, 'but that's water under the bridge now. I'm surprised to see you in Edinburgh,' he admitted.

'It isn't all that odd,' she said. 'I've an assignment at the Festival as a stage designer which has to be finished by June and then I'm going on to Rome. I seem to have the Midas touch at the moment,' she smiled, 'so I hope it will last.' She put her empty mug down on the table between them. 'Kate and I were discussing the future,' she added deliberately, 'so I'll leave her to tell you all about it, because I really must go. I have a heavy date for lunch and a meeting with a Festival V.I.P. afterwards.'

Charles stood aside for her to pass.

'I hope you'll be successful in your new career,' he said stiffly.

Katherine went to the flat door with Coralie.

'Will you settle in Rome?' she asked.

'Good heavens, no!' Coralie's eyes were shining as she looked into the future. 'Rome will only be the beginning. If I do well there I'll be able to establish an international reputation and then it will be back to New York to work there for a year or two or even to Los Angeles. I'd like to work in L.A. sooner or later,' she added thoughtfully. 'It's Mecca as far as I'm concerned.'

The hardness which Katherine had glimpsed in her before was more obvious now and she was eager to get away.

'Must dash!' she said. 'Good luck with Charles!'

She had no idea of the havoc she had wrought, of the web of deceit she had spun reaching out to entangle other people's lives, and as she banged the outside door behind her Katherine could almost hear her laughter echoing up the staircase.

Charles was washing up the mugs in the kitchen.

'I didn't—invite Coralie to come,' she said, standing just inside the door. 'She came because she said she had to speak to somebody and she knew Emma and I had been staying here because she asked me when she came to the gallery.'

He turned slowly, something in his expression which she could not fathom.

'I'm not interested in Coralie's reasons for being here, Kate,' he said. 'I came because I wanted to know what you're going to do.'

'I'm—looking for a job.'

He followed her through to the living-room.

'Is that what you really want?'

She had never heard him speak so softly before.

'It's what I must do.'

Katherine busied herself with the ridiculous non-essentials of rearranging the cushions on the settee and flicking imaginary dust from the highly-polished surface of the tables while he looked about him at the changes she had made in a room which had once been austere, smiling a little when he saw the flowers in the kitchen bowl which was all she could find.

'I've made a start,' she said breathlessly, indicating the copy of *The Scotsman* which lay folded on the side table. 'There are plenty of situations vacant when you look for them and I've phoned my name in to an agency.'

'Even though a job as a secretary may be the very last thing you want?' She felt his hands strong on her shoulders as he turned her round to face him. 'Look at me, Kate,' he commanded. 'Almost the last time I saw you you said you were in love.'

As the hot colour of embarrassment flooded into her cheeks she could no longer look away from his demanding eyes.

'I was angry——' she began.

'Do you have to be angry to say you love me?' His tone was slightly amused as he let his arms slip round her, drawing her strongly towards him. 'Say it again, Kate,' he commanded, 'so that I can be sure it's true.'

She stood quite still, hardly believing that all this was really happening, having to convince herself that Charles was asking for her love instead of telling her to go. Then, because she hadn't answered him, he swept her into his arms, kissing her with a passion which seemed to shake him to the foundations of his being. No cold, disdainful kisses these, but kisses full of promise and hope.

'I thought you'd never believe me about Coralie,' she whispered, at last. 'I thought you'd never want to see me again.'

He held her close.

'I don't think we need to worry about Coralie any more,' he said, his lips close against her hair. 'It didn't take me long after you came to Glassary to realise how different you were, though I'd misjudged you at first. There was nothing hard about you, although you had every right to tell me what you thought about me. I behaved pretty badly,' he admitted, 'but Sandy means a lot to us at Glassary. We knew Coralie would cheat again when she felt like it, but I was determined to bring Sandy back for my brother's sake. I owe Fergus my life, you see. He wouldn't be like he is now if he hadn't pulled me out of a blazing plane and been caught in the wreckage as it blew up.' His arms tightened as his thoughts slid into the past. 'I thought he was in love with you when you first came to the glen, and that seemed to be the answer to a good many things until that day on the moor when we were caught by the mist. I knew then that I wanted you more than anything in the world, only there was Fergus. You were kind and helpful and he could so easily have fallen in love after all he'd been through, so it was up to me to stand aside.'

'He'd fallen in love long before that,' Katherine whispered. 'Didn't you know about Emma?'

He kissed her forehead.

'It's funny how we all took Emma for granted,' he said. 'She's always been "the girl next door" and it's amazing how blind you can be when you try to convince yourself that you're not interested in love.' He looked over her head at the tidy room. 'I suppose someone has told you about Deirdre?' he asked.

'I found her photograph,' Katherine admitted, stirring in his arms. 'It was in one of the bedroom drawers. Afterwards I wondered why you'd kept it hidden away there for so long.'

'To remind me,' he said harshly. 'I spent three years regretting Deirdre, wishing we'd never met yet half believing I was still in love with her. Then, when I knew there were no scars left, I hung on to her portrait as a reminder of how treacherous a woman could be.'

She held him back from her a little.

'I knew you thought that when we first met,' she told him gently. 'There was a guarded look about you, that vague contempt, but it wasn't fair to judge everyone by a first disappointment. It was natural enough, I suppose,' she conceded, 'when you found I had taken Sandy because you had only Coralie and Deirdre to judge me by, but now—but now all that doesn't matter! I can't believe I'm here in your arms and we've found each other at last!'

'For good,' he said tenderly. 'Coralie phoned Fergus yesterday, by the way,' he added as he led her through the hall towards the flat door, 'offering to abide by the letter of the law. If she sees Sandy occasionally she'll be content and she'll have a successful career into the bargain,' he added dryly.

'She came here to say much the same thing to me,' Katherine admitted. 'Only she was really concerned about the decision she'd made. She was still not convinced that it was the right one and she was almost in tears because she wasn't sure. She had tried to work it out, but I think she knew in the end that her career had to come first.'

'I wouldn't be surprised if she knew that in the beginning,' Charles said uncharitably. 'She made Fergus's life a veritable hell with her indecisions and after Sandy was born she didn't want to know.'

'She loved him,' Katherine protested. 'She must have loved her own child.'

'One part of her may have done, but it wasn't her major concern,' he decided. 'She was obsessed by success even before she married Fergus, but it was love at first sight as far as he was concerned and they married within a month of meeting each other. Then, when Sandy was born, Coralie found out what she'd done. She'd sold her precious freedom down the river, and that was more than she could take. She's tremendously talented—I'm not arguing against that—but she could have seen Fergus through his particular ordeal before she went off to indulge herself elsewhere.'

'I wish it could have worked out better for you all.' They had halted beside the stack of unsold paintings. 'The exhibition has been a—sort of compensation for Fergus, hasn't it? And Emma has done well, too.'

'She's elated in her own quiet way,' Charles agreed.

'Coralie saw them together at the gallery when Fergus came back there with Sandy from the Zoo. I think that's what finally sealed her decision,' Katherine said. 'She saw him happy and contented, a normal little boy in a caring atmosphere where he could grow up without complications. It must have been very difficult for her, Charles, and it's something we have to understand.'

'It's going to take me quite a while,' he admitted, 'but meantime I have to get this lot back to Glassary.' He looked down at the paintings. 'Where have you left your car?'

'Just round the corner.' She watched as he sorted out the canvases. 'Did you come by air?'

He nodded.

'I flew down with the Cessna.' His mouth lifted in a one-sided smile. 'I was short of time.'

'Then I can drive you to the airport?'

'That was the idea,' he agreed. 'I'll go ahead with this

lot and you can follow with the others. I'd offer you lunch,' he added as she opened the door, 'but private aircraft, no matter how small, cost money while they're standing on a municipal airstrip.'

She thought of his swift transition to the glen, longing to go with him, but he had said so little about the future. Just that he loved her and her thoughts had stopped there. It was almost as if the whole world had stopped revolving while he had kissed her without restraint and she had responded as eagerly to his ardent caress.

He passed her on the stairs coming back up.

'Is that the lot?' he asked.

'Everything except my personal belongings,' she agreed. 'My case was already packed when Coralie appeared.'

Charles made no reply to that, but when he came down to join her in the foyer he was carrying her suitcase and her coat. Apparently he didn't want her to go back to the flat.

Some of the radiance faded from her eyes.

'I'll get my handbag,' she said, 'and the keys.'

She had already given him the key of her car and when she went back to the flat she allowed herself a few minutes to say goodbye. She had been happy here working so closely with such dedicated spirits as Emma and Fergus and feeling that she was gradually coming to understand Charles in spite of their initial misunderstanding.

The bedroom door was slightly ajar and she noticed that one of the drawers in the dressing-chest had been opened. Crossing to it automatically, she realised that it was the drawer in which she had buried Deirdre's photograph among all the tissue paper, but now the drawer was empty. All the other drawers were as she had left them, so she could only conclude that Charles had taken the photograph of his former love to dispose of it in some other way.

Her car was drawn up at the kerb when she closed the outer door behind her, feeling that she had shut it on a dark track of Charles's life.

'I'm not going to need a taxi, after all,' he said. 'I've got everything into the boot and we can put the rest on the back seat.'

'I see you're going to drive,' she smiled as he remained behind the steering-wheel. 'Surely you can trust me!'

'Implicitly! But I have my reservations about being driven by a woman. Besides,' he added, smiling broadly, 'this is a first-class kidnapping. I can't afford to let you slip through my fingers a second time.'

'Charles!' Her heart was beating very fast as she got in beside him. 'Does it mean you want me to come to Glassary?'

'It means I'm *taking* you to Glassary,' he said, letting in the clutch. 'Where else? I told you it was a first-class kidnapping!'

'You can't call it that when the victim is so eager to go!' Katherine put a hand on his arm. 'Oh, Charles, it's so difficult for me to believe! I should have had a little more time.'

'Time doesn't exist,' he said. 'Not when you're thinking of a timeless future. Have you ever flown in a small plane before?'

'Never.' She felt quite breathless. 'I've a notion I might be terrified!'

'You can hold on to my arm!'

They left her car in the airport parking lot when they had packed everything in the Cesna and Charles had completed the necessary formalities before take-off. Dwarfed by the giant jet-propelled aircraft waiting to travel to the farthest corners of the earth, the little blue-and-white plane looked like a hovering bird as they taxied down the runway, but soon they were airborne and flying into the sun. Katherine felt the lift as the wheels left the tarmac and the magic of the first moment of flight as the earth dwindled beneath them and the Pentland Hills became no more than a ruffle on its surface, and then they were leaving the blue expanse of the Firth behind them and travelling west along the line of the river with the smoke of industry far beneath them and the mountains of the north and west directly ahead.

'Coming home must always be like this for you, Charles,' she said, aware of the keenness in him as he looked down on a wide strath between the soaring peaks.

'I wanted you to see it like this,' he said, turning towards her. 'You're not nervous?'

She shook her head.

'It's going to be over all too soon,' she declared. 'It's lovely to look down on the world like this.'

'*Our* world,' he corrected as he pointed out the narrow ribbon of Loch Earn glittering in the sun, with the white sails of little yachts dotting its surface like resting birds. 'We'll soon be home.'

'It's like being on a magic carpet,' she said fancifully as they glided close to the mountainsides, finding their way from glen to glen, and then there was another stretch of water and another glen before she realised that they were gliding slowly down to land.

'It's over so soon,' she regretted. 'Look! I can see Glassary and the loch! I can even see the Stable House and the road over the bridge!'

Charles circled to bring it all in close.

'Do you think you could stay here for the rest of your life?' he asked quietly. 'It wouldn't be a prison, Kate, or even a fortress, as you once imagined. It would be a life apart, dedicated to Glassary, but the outside world wouldn't be so far away. You can see for yourself how quickly we've come from Edinburgh. You would never need to feel—restricted or left out in any way. Even by car it's a short enough journey and there's always plenty to do.'

She leaned forward to put her hand over his.

'Don't make excuses for Glassary,' she said gently. 'I'll always love it, and besides, there'll be Emma and Sandy and Fergus—and so many people I have yet to meet.'

Before he set the controls for the short approach down the glen he said:

'I've got some news for you, come to think of it! Emma and Fergus will be married just as soon as Mrs Falkland can get extra help in the hotel. It will be a very quiet affair,' he added, 'but you and I will have to be prepared for something quite different, Kate. We owe the glen a pukka wedding with all the trimmings, I'm afraid.' He held her hand to his lips. 'Will you mind very much?'

'I'd even do that for Glassary!' she smiled, kissing his cheek as his eyes narrowed in concentration for the final approach to the narrow grass runway beside the loch. 'I'd do anything for you both.'

The little plane touched down, bumping to a standstill at the very edge of the loch and Sandy came running from the Stable House with Emma and Fergus in his wake.

'Welcome home!' said Fergus, though a breathless Sandy had reached them first. 'Welcome home to Glassary!'

Harlequin® Plus

A WORD ABOUT THE AUTHOR

Jean S. MacLeod, one of Harlequin's most established authors, has been writing since before World War II. The ideas and the words still pour out as fresh and romantic as ever. As Jean explains; "My writing has been some sort of lifeline—something to turn to in times of stress, something that has meant friendships in far places and a full generous life at home."

Born in Glasgow, Scotland, she began her writing career as an author of serialized novels for a popular Scottish women's magazine. She was married in Newcastle upon Tyne, England, but returned to Scotland during the war. Engaged in air-raid warden duties, she guarded the Holy Loch, which was at that time a British submarine base.

After the war she and her family settled in Yorkshire. Mills & Boon, Harlequin's sister company, eventually became her publisher, and Jean found herself traveling up and down the country, speaking to women's groups, lecturing to writers' circles and appearing on television. She also began to travel abroad, making numerous new friends in the United States and Canada.

Today, "many thousands of words later," the wheel has turned full circle. Jean has returned to live in her beloved Scotland.

Jean S. MacLeod's first Harlequin Romance was *The Silent Valley* (#431), which was published in 1958. This was followed by *Dear Doctor Everett* (#434), *Air Ambulance* (#451) and an incredible string of successes that include such always popular titles as *Bleak Heritage* (#1440), *Time Suspended* (#1845) and *Island Stranger* (#2142).

Harlequin Presents...